I PICK YOU

SIGNS OF LIFE SERIES
BOOK 3

CRESTON MAPES

ROOFTOP

STAND-ALONE THRILLERS

I Am In Here

Nobody

SIGNS OF LIFE SERIES

Signs of Life

Let My Daughter Go

I Pick You

Charm Artist

Son & Shield

Secrets in Shadows

THE CRITTENDON FILES

Fear Has a Name

Poison Town

Sky Zone

ROCK STAR CHRONICLES

Dark Star: Confessions of a Rock Idol

Full Tilt

going to want Creston to write a follow up book on each of the characters." **Gregg Hart**

"He's only got a year remaining 'til retirement, but veteran Portland PD investigator, Wayne Deetz finally may have met his match. And with *I Pick You*, celebrated suspense author Creston Mapes keeps his thumb placed firmly on the pulse of current culture—delivering a thrilling third installment in his popular 'Signs of Life Series.'" **Author Christopher Long**

This is a work of fiction. Names, characters, organizations, places, events, and incidents are either products of the author's imagination or are used fictitiously. Any resemblance to actual persons, living or dead, or actual events is purely coincidental.

No part of this book may be reproduced or stored in a retrieval system, or transmitted in any form or by any means, electronic, mechanical, photocopying, recording, or otherwise, without express written permission of the publisher.

*Dedicated to Chuck Pardoe and Steve Vibert
for your off-the-charts creative input.*

*Thanks to Patty, editor extraordinaire,
and my amazing early reader team!*

1

THE FRONT DOOR of the small yellow house opened before Portland PD Investigator Wayne Deetz had even put his Subaru in park. Family friend Callie Freeland walked through the door and swiftly made her way down the front steps with her arms crossed, toward Deetz's slowing car. She'd phoned him fifteen minutes earlier and said she was at a friend's house—a friend who was in trouble.

Deetz parked at the curb, got out, rounded the car and headed up the driveway. It was chilly and gray, a typical fall Oregon weekday morning. Deetz met Callie on the sidewalk in front of the house. The garage door was closed. Callie's Volkswagen was parked in the driveway.

"Thanks for coming Wayne." Callie gave him a quick hug and bundled up her thick navy sweater. "I hope I did the right thing, calling you."

"Better safe than sorry. What's going on?"

Callie had shut the front door and obviously wanted to talk to Deetz alone before they went in.

"The friend who lives here is Sunny Carlisle. Single. About my age . . . Sorry I'm talking so fast—you'll see why. Anyway, she works at City Hall, some administrative job. Wonderful person. We met at aerobics class a few months ago. She's become a good friend.

Anyway, she dates this guy, Blaine Milligan . . . I've never met him, but he sounds like trouble."

"Go on."

"You know I volunteer at the Dorcas House in town—the domestic violence shelter?"

"Sure, yeah." Deetz said, recalling Callie herself had been the victim of domestic abuse several years earlier. She'd fled to the Dorcas House after the last straw when the guy had broken her nose. Ironically, he got gunned down in the infamous Pioneer Square massacre of 2018.

"So, I know the signs, Wayne. Sunny hasn't come right out and told me that Blaine abuses her, but I'm almost certain he is. I've seen bruising. She's always on edge, on alert. Chronic apprehension. Plus, I feel like she's been dropping me hints, kind of like a cry for help."

"Okay, so what's happening right now? Are they in there?" He nodded toward the house.

"He's not here, but he's coming. I was picking Sunny up to get coffee and go shopping. When I got here, she suddenly said she couldn't go. She's a nervous wreck. Says Blaine is upset about something and is on his way here. She wants me to leave. I knew you were close . . . I hope you don't mind. I can't call Tyson—he's in school. And you're the law . . ."

"Of course, I don't mind. I was on my way into the office anyway." Deetz hesitated, wrestling with how to proceed. "Did you want me to just be here, in my car, in case anything happens? Or, what are you thinking?"

"I don't even know, Wayne." Callie looked around nervously, as if watching for Blaine's car. "I just know from firsthand experience what can happen."

"I know you do."

"I'm scared for her."

"Did you want me to go inside? Be here when he gets here?"

The front door opened. A pretty young Black woman stepped out. "Callie? What's going on? I thought you were leaving?"

Callie whispered to Deetz, "Let's just walk up there." She began walking and Deetz started along with her, a bit hesitant about the whole thing.

"Callie?" Sunny called and threw up her hands as if to ask what was going on.

Callie chuckled and called up to Sunny. "I want you to meet a friend of mine. He was in the neighborhood . . ."

"I can't right now," Sunny said. "I've really got to go."

Callie kept walking and Deetz went along.

"This is my good friend, Wayne Deetz. He's with the Portland Police."

Sunny's small mouth dropped open. She had beautiful shiny black hair, straightened, but with a wave in it, about shoulder length.

Deetz put his hand out. "Pleased to meet you, Sunny."

Sunny said hello and gave Deetz a quick shake, but barely made eye contact. She checked the street in front of the house, back and forth.

"Wayne's the one I told you about. He led the investigation in the Pioneer Square shootings."

Sunny nodded. "I think I recognize you—from the news."

"Oh, yeah. Big local celebrity." Callie snickered. Deetz could tell she, too, was nervous.

"Listen, it's great to meet you," Sunny said, sharply. "I'm sorry. I've got to run." She backed away. She was thin and lanky, built like a volleyball player. She wore khaki pants and a green sweater. "My boyfriend's due any minute. Some urgent business." She feigned a laugh and began walking back toward the front door.

"Maybe I should stay and finally meet the famous Blaine Milligan," Callie said, almost in desperation.

Sunny chuckled again, waved, and kept walking. "Next time, next time, for sure. I'll see you guys."

She went in the house and the door nudged shut.

Callie and Deetz looked at each other. He began walking back down the sidewalk.

"There's not much more you can do," Deetz said.

"I've got a bad feeling about this." Callie walked extremely slowly, stalling. They got to her car and stared at each other.

"You probably think I'm crazy," she said.

"Not at all," Deetz said. "But she's an adult. She's making this decision. She obviously doesn't want us here."

"Alright." Callie huffed, shook her head, and dug her keys out of her shoulder bag. "I guess I've done all I can." She was still hesitant. "Thanks so much for coming, Wayne. It means a lot."

"No problem at all. Let me know if there's anything else I can do." He looked at the house. "Keep me posted on this."

Deetz headed down the driveway toward his car. He had a lot on his mind, including the current racial tensions that had the city in an uproar. It was his first week back on the job in six weeks. His boss, Sergeant Dolby Tidwell, had suspended him without pay for barging into the home of Hunter Tranton—the teenage suspect in his daughter Leena's kidnapping. This was *after* Deetz had been taken off the case. He'd known it was wrong, but Leena was missing and the Tranton kid was the lead suspect. To make matters worse, Deetz had entered the home with his two sons, J.P., 24, and Brandon, 22, the latter of whom discharged his firearm twice in the mansion, destroying a massive chandelier.

Deetz made it to his car, got in, started it, and sat there, figuring he'd wait a few more minutes to see if this Blaine character showed up. He checked his email on his phone.

Callie was taking her time leaving, but finally got to the bottom of the driveway. She stopped, checked both ways, waved, and took off.

Her fiancé, Tyson Cooper, had gone with Deetz and his sons the night they'd tracked Leena down at the Pacific Point Shipping Yard along the Willamette River. Thank God Tyson had been there. It had turned into a shootout. They were lucky to be alive. Deetz still couldn't believe they'd found Leena all in one piece. She'd been sold in a human trafficking deal and was about to be shipped to Shanghai. He gave thanks silently for the thousandth time.

He checked his rearview mirror and the street in front of him: nothing. He looked at his watch and decided to wait three more minutes before taking off for police headquarters.

Willow Weston—the mastermind in the Portland shootings and in the kidnapping of Leena and another local teenager, Kelsey Stonegate—was in jail still awaiting trial. Whether Leena and Kelsey would be called to testify was yet to be determined. Leena kept telling Deetz and Joanie she was excited to go to court. They could only chuckle at her innocence. Kelsey, on the other hand, was still struggling mightily with PTSD, was undergoing intense ther-apy, and had not gone back to school. In fact, she'd not been back out in public at all.

Deetz and Leena had gone to visit her several times at the Stonegate home and both times Kelsey wore a weighted vest and sat huddled up in the front room with all the blinds closed. But her parents insisted she loved Leena's visits. Leena shared Bible verses she'd written down for Kelsey, and her parents said she clung to them for days after her visits.

Willow's delinquent accomplices, Brady Mann and Hunter Tran-ton, were also in jail awaiting trial. Hunter's father was out on bond but was facing charges of obstructing justice in Leena's disappear-ance. The whole thing was going to be one huge legal showdown. Officials were still trying to decide if all of those charged could get a fair trial in the city of Portland.

The worst thing about Deetz's suspension had been that the days he was off had not counted toward his retirement. He and Joanie had been counting down the days. He was about fourteen months away from hitting his thirty-five year mark and receiving a generous pension. He smiled thinking about the colorful paper chain Joanie had created. His instructions were to tear off one ring each day until his final day. She'd told him just that morning he had four hundred fourteen days to go.

He glanced at the time, put the Subaru in drive and looked back over his shoulder before pulling out. A vehicle was approaching with its blinker on. Deetz stopped and waited to see if it might be the boyfriend.

Within a few seconds, the vehicle—a towering white pickup truck—had slowed and was right next to him, about to turn into the driveway. It did so and stopped close to Deetz, at the base of the driveway. Deetz always wondered what anyone needed with such massive vehicles; they barely fit on the road, let alone in parking spaces.

The Caucasian driver, who Deetz assumed was Blaine Milligan, leaned way over the passenger seat—toward Deetz—with an arm resting atop the steering wheel. With the reflection in the windows, Deetz couldn't really make him out. Then the passenger window buzzed down. The guy glared at Deetz as if he'd just tried to run him off the road, then threw up his hands and yelled something. Deetz sat still, wondering if Sunny had called the guy and told him Deetz was a cop? But that didn't make sense. What if he *was* a cop? Deetz and this guy had no past.

When Deetz didn't move a muscle, the guy's door banged open and he was around the long truck in seconds, taking five-foot strides.

Deetz's heart rate ticked up as he put his car in park.

"What the heck do you think you're doin'?" The guy was all mass and bone. He had wavy blackish gray hair and a five o'clock shadow. He got to Deetz's window and ripped off his sunglasses. His eyes were bloodshot.

Deetz slowly moved his hand to the remote button and put his window down.

The guy was hot. "Who are you and what business do you have parking here? This is private property."

Deetz squinted at him, a bit shaken, debating how much information to divulge.

"I'm talkin' to you, old man. *Speak up!*"

Slowly, Deetz reached inside his coat, got his leather badge case, opened it and held it up, about to say something.

"I don't care who the heck you are, man. You don't park in front of this house. Now get the heck out of here before I smash your face in."

The guy was in overdrive.

Deetz's adrenaline was pumping.

He feared for Sunny.

He reached for the remote again, put the window up, and shoved his door open.

2

———————

Deetz got out of the car and slowly drew his Glock.

Blaine's dark eyes widened, his huge hands shot up, he stepped back—and smirked.

Deetz said, "Since you're a friend of a friend, I'm going to ignore your impoliteness this one time. My name's Wayne Deetz, Portland PD. A very dear friend of mine knows the nice lady who lives here. In fact, we were all just visiting a minute ago."

Blaine glanced at the house, put his hands down, and stepped closer to Deetz. "If you're talking about Callie Freeland, she ain't no friend. In fact, you can give her a message—"

"That may be so, but she *is* a good friend of the woman who lives here—"

"The woman who *lives here* is *my* girlfriend, Cop Daddy. And she is none of your business, or Callie Freeland's. Now, why don't you take your little gun and your little Jap piece of tin car and go down to the donut shop for your free coffee?"

The guy was like a steel wall. And he wasn't budging.

Deetz could feel his pulse ticking in his temples. But he kept his cool.

"If your demeanor this morning is any indication, *Blaine*, then I think I have a very good reason to keep my eye on you. That is your name, right? Blaine Milligan? And the woman who resides here is Sunny Carlisle, correct?"

Blaine stepped even closer to Deetz, into his personal space, way too close. Deetz could smell his strong aftershave.

"Let's get something clear. I don't care *who* you are. I'm telling you to stay away. Keep out of our business. I can find out where you live, Deetz, was it? Wayne Deetz? Two can play this game, Cop Daddy. Trust me, you don't want to mess with me."

Deetz was just old enough to have lost all patience with the evil people he had to confront each day—especially when they threatened to step over boundaries into his personal life.

"Maybe you want to go to police headquarters right now with me, hmm?" Deetz waved his gun at the guy. "We can punch in your name, see what comes up in the database?"

Blaine heaved his rock-solid chest into Deetz, bashing him, surprising him, and walking past toward his truck. He wore a short-sleeved button down shirt, faded jeans, and dark steel-toed boots. A thick chain hung from his belt and the watch on his thick wrist was huge. Everything about the guy pulsed on steroids.

He yanked open the door, stopped, and stared back at Deetz. "I would have thought as long as you've been on the force you would have learned your lesson about guys like me—the crazy ones? I'm the type you need to just let go, Deetz. Turn the other way. You made a dangerous mistake coming here. But you're in my world now. Better watch your back—and tell Callie Freeland to do the same."

Deetz was about to warn him about making threats, but Blaine hoisted himself into the cab of his truck in a flash. The door slammed and the vehicle rumbled backward, bounced into the street, and roared off.

Deetz took his glasses off, leaned both forearms against the top of the Subaru, and sighed.

He was shaking slightly.

It was nutcases like Blaine Milligan who made him long for retirement.

Four hundred fourteen days . . .

It was good Blaine didn't go inside the house just then; who knew what he would have done to Sunny? But Deetz feared for her, especially now, because he'd gone and blabbed to Blaine that he'd stood out there and talked with Sunny and Callie.

Deetz got his phone out and rang Callie. He explained what had happened with Blaine.

"I need to call Sunny and warn her," Callie said. "Are you still there?"

"I'm here." He looked up at the house, debating whether to go talk to Sunny.

"Let me call you right back," Callie said.

"Have you told Sunny about the shelter, where you volunteer?"

"Oh yeah, I mention it often—so she knows there's a place she can go. But she's never come right out and told me he abuses her. We're working toward that, I think."

"Is he a drinker? Mental issues? What's the deal? Because, I mean, he was wired."

"She says he's bipolar."

"On meds?"

"On and off. That's part of the problem. She says he hates taking them cuz they make him feel like a blob."

"Better a blob than a raging maniac . . . Sorry, I shouldn't say that. But he was a real jerk. Dangerous."

"So, are you leaving?" Callie said.

"I'm thinking about going to the door."

Callie didn't say anything. She was probably hoping he would get involved.

Deetz looked at the time. He needed to get to the office, but he also felt an obligation to try to help Sunny.

"Well, let me know what you're going to do, cuz if you're not going to talk to her, I'm going to give her a heads-up," Callie said.

He made up his mind. "Don't call her. I'll talk to her now."

"Thank you, Wayne."

"Certainly. Listen. He mentioned your name and what he said wasn't very nice."

"Here's what I think," Callie said. "This is almost embarrassing, but I think he's jealous of me. Remember I told you we were going for coffee today, Sunny and me?"

"Yes."

"I honestly feel like he found out and was jealous—that's why he was coming home in a rage. Sunny's mentioned before he's weird about her friends and her phone, which to me spells hyper-jealousy."

"All right, I'm going to go talk to her. I'll let you know what happens." He locked the car and headed up the driveway.

"Thank you, Wayne."

"Listen, I think you need to stay out of the picture for a while, at least till this blows over. If he's jealous of you, that's not good."

"I've never even met the guy."

"Believe me, with this type of guy, it doesn't matter. Just stay clear for a while. I wouldn't talk to her for a bit if I was you."

"Okay, we'll see," Callie said. "Let me know how it goes."

"Will do."

SUNNY WAS in tears when she pulled the front door open.

"May I come in?" Deetz said.

Her watery brown eyes darted back and forth toward the street in front of the house. She stood with a tissue waded tight in her fist, arms crossed, almost shivering. "I'll come out." Sunny stepped out the front door and continued looking around.

"Fine." Deetz backed up, thinking this wasn't a good sign. She was scared to even let a police officer inside for fear of the wrath of Blaine Milligan.

"I met Blaine a few minutes ago," Deetz said.

"I saw."

"Does his temper always run so hot?"

Sunny just stared at him. The whites of her big eyes were stunning. Her lips were full and pretty. Deetz guessed her to be in her late twenties, like Callie. Blaine Milligan looked older, perhaps mid-thirties.

When she didn't answer, he forged ahead. "Do you know why I came here this morning?"

"Did Callie call you?"

Deetz nodded. "She's concerned about you, Sunny. She's concerned about your relationship with Blaine."

Sunny's head dropped. "I thought so." Her shoulders lurched slightly as more emotion churned to the surface. Her feet shifted.

"If he's hurting you in any way—physically, mentally—you need to get away from him," Deetz said. "Is this your house?"

She nodded quickly, set her shoulders back, and took in a deep breath.

"Does he live here with you?" Deetz said.

"Sometimes," she blurted, trying to hold back the tears.

"Sunny, if he's harming you, we can get a restraining order so he can't come near you."

She smirked and shook her head, then looked up at the white sky. "You don't understand."

"Tell me this—"

"He doesn't obey the law. He wouldn't stay away. No one tells him anything. He's not scared of anything. Nothing and no one can stop him from doing whatever he wants."

"Sunny, is he hurting you?"

She sniffed in another choppy breath and her eyes rolled up to the sky. "It's too involved. There's too much to explain." She looked back at the street. "You really shouldn't be here. He'll be back soon."

Deetz nodded. "I know it can seem like there's no way out, but believe me, there are ways out and you need to get out, if you are being abused. If you tell me what's going on, I can help."

Her mouth sealed shut, her jaw jutted forward, and her whole lean body trembled. She shook her head. "You should go. Please."

"Sunny—"

"He's nearby. I know it. You should definitely go. I don't want to see anybody get hurt."

"Callie's told you about the shelter where she volunteers, right? Dorcas House? It's in a confidential, safe location. It's for domestic violence survivors. They offer free counseling and support services. Blaine can never find you there."

"He would," she blurted. "That's what no one understands. That's what's too hard to explain to anyone. He *would* find me. He's not like other people. He breaks the rules. And then . . ." She cried.

Something startled her and her head swiveled to the inside of the house. "That's him. He's calling." She looked at Deetz. "Please go and just drop this. Don't come back. Thank you. Thank you, anyway." She dashed inside.

The door swung closed, but remained ajar a few inches. Deetz stepped closer and listened.

"I did not call him, Blaine. He's a friend of Callie's. He just showed up!"

Deetz remained with his ear to the door.

"I have no idea. I haven't told anyone anything about us, or you. I promise, Blaine. You have to believe me."

There was a long pause.

"Don't do that, Blaine. She didn't mean any harm," Sunny said. "If you've got a problem, take it out on me. Our relationship is no one else's business . . . I swear, I haven't said anything to anyone! Callie volunteers at a women's shelter. She suspects something. I can't help it. I'm doing my best . . . Please don't do that. Please, just leave my friends alone."

Sunny was begging him now. Sobbing.

Then Deetz heard footsteps and the door slammed shut in his face.

3

———————

As she drove from Sunny's back into Portland city limits amidst remnants of the morning rush hour, Callie admittedly felt sorry for herself. She'd worked her normal nightshift at the warehouse the night before and had only gotten about two hours sleep that morning before getting up to meet Sunny—and then Blaine had rained on their parade.

When she spotted an open parking space in front of her favorite coffee shop, she took it, ran in, and treated herself to a special hot tea she couldn't get anyplace else. She debated going shopping by herself, but decided to head back to her apartment and catch some sleep. After all, she had to work again that night. She tipped the barista, talked to a woman she recognized from work, and got back on the road.

Reflecting on the morning's events, Callie was more convinced than ever God had brought her together with Sunny at aerobics class for a purpose. After all, Callie not only volunteered at a domestic violence shelter, she herself had been a victim of some very dark physical and mental abuse. In fact, she'd escaped to the Dorcas House back in 2018 to get away from the wrath of her then boyfriend, Keith Ramsey.

She still loathed herself for falling in love with Keith, a handsome charmer on the exterior. Popular. Successful. The Portland bachelor everyone admired. For a full year, she kept telling herself he was the one, that his temper tantrums were a passing thing—but the cruelty and physical abuse only got darker and more violent as time went on. And the terror was magnified when he drank.

Callie could clearly see her former self in Sunny. Agitated. Humiliated. Controlled. Hopeless. Nervous. Beaten down. As she drove, she literally got cold with chills remembering the day Keith had drank too much, gotten jealous of her pastor, of all people, and ended up breaking her nose and cracking four of her ribs.

In hindsight, that turned out to be the best day of her life, because it was the day she finally made up her mind to leave—and she fled to the Dorcas House.

She never saw Keith Ramsey alive again.

Callie flipped on the heat. Her eyes filled with tears as she kept the VW steady in her lane.

She'd lived in secrecy at the Dorcas House for two weeks. She hadn't told her parents or four brothers. The staff and volunteers had loved her unconditionally, listened to her, counseled her, supported her and, most of all, helped her begin to understand that her past with Keith did not define who she was or what her future would look like.

The days she stayed at the Dorcas House were also nerve-wracking and dicey. Word on the street was that Keith was livid Callie had taken off—and was searching high and low for her. A friend told her later Keith had gone berserk trying to track her down. She said he'd threatened to kill Callie and himself when he found her.

He would have done it. I know he would have.

But then May seventh happened.

A nineteen-year-old named Rogan Sneed opened fire at Pioneer Square in Portland with an assault rifle, killing twenty-one people. Keith Ramsey had been one of the first to drop to the red bricks that day.

She wiped her eyes and thought of Tyson.

He'd lost his wife that day, too. Kim. Fortunately, they hadn't had children.

Callie met Tyson weeks later on the nightshift at the warehouse. After the massacre, he'd quit his high school teaching job and become an angry recluse, working through the night, avoiding people, meeting with a psychiatrist, and trying to figure out how the God he once loved could be so cruel.

But then they met.

She chuckled thinking about how she was the one who'd started their tradition of calling each other by their last names—Freeland and Cooper.

They still did it.

She looked down at the engagement ring he'd presented to her last summer. A shiny, thick platinum band with a solitary diamond. The inscription inside the band read, "Ever Onward," something his mom used to say, and that they'd come to say after having been through so much pain and tragedy.

She thought back to the one-year anniversary of the Portland shooting. There'd been a vigil and time of remembrance at Pioneer Square and she'd invited Tyson. He hadn't wanted to go. She was meeting friends from her little church.

He did come after all.

Thank God.

She shook her head in disbelief, remembering how a copycat shooter, twenty-seven year-old Daniel Bay Tinker, had emerged in the crowd nearby. He was about to start firing on people at will. Detective Deetz was on his way from across the courtyard, but was too far away in the crowd to stop the guy. Callie's heart beat faster as she recalled Tyson ripping a large black gun from inside his jacket and practically knocking her down to the pavement, yelling at her to stay close to him. On one knee with the gun locked in front of him, Tyson fired repeatedly, killing Tinker and saving dozens of lives.

She reached over and got a napkin from the glove compartment and wiped her eyes.

She and Tyson both lost people at the original massacre in 2018. They'd both gone through hell. And, by God's mercy, they'd then found each other.

They were to be married next spring.

That, too, gave her chills—and a smile.

What an emotional mess she was.

Lack of sleep.

She wished she could call Tyson and tell him about what

happened with Sunny that morning, but he was back at his old job teaching geography at Wendell Brock High School.

She glanced at her phone to see if she'd heard from Wayne, but she hadn't. She worried for Sunny, wondering if Blaine had come back.

Her phone vibrated. It was Deetz.

"Hi, Wayne," she answered.

"Hey Callie. So, I went up to the door. Sunny came out. We talked. She didn't admit anything, but she did break down, got emotional. I gave her options, like Dorcas House, restraining order . . . She's obviously scared."

"Right? Now I know I'm not imagining all this."

He told her about how Blaine called Sunny toward the end of his visit and put her on the defensive.

"She's convinced he would flat out ignore any kind of restraining order. Having met him, I believe it," Deetz said.

"What's he like?"

"Big. Mean. Crazy."

"Great."

"Yeah."

"She told me he doesn't live there all the time," Callie said. "He sounds like an uninvited houseguest who pops in whenever he feels like it. He can leave for weeks, she thinks he's out of her life, she lets her guard down, and he comes steamrolling back in again, owning the place, owning her—like he was never gone. I may have it all wrong. Tyson says I'm way too suspicious."

"She's never officially gone to the police?" Deetz said.

"No. She won't admit what's happening. I know what it's like. He cries and apologizes, brings flowers, and she thinks it'll be different next time, and it never is."

"Hmm. I hate to say it but she's got to be the one who does something. You can't make her get out of there. And, like I said, you need to keep your distance. That guy's no one to mess with."

"Wayne, I've got to do something. I'm afraid he's really going to hurt her. Isn't there someone I can call within the police or isn't there some kind of adult protective services?"

"That's for elderly people being abused—over sixty, I think," Deetz said. "There's a Domestic Violence Division within the city government, but again, Sunny would need to contact them, file a report. Then they could help her get a restraining order."

"Maybe I could call them and have a case worker visit her?"

"I'm not sure about that, Callie. You could ask. You could also search online. I think there's some kind of women's crisis line. You could call and talk to them."

"That's what I'm going to do. I'll do it when I get home. Thanks again, Wayne. How's everything with Joanie and the gang?"

"No complaints. Everyone's healthy. J.P.'s working in PR for a big coffee distributor. His Tammy is still in social work. Brandon's a senior in college and he's got an internship with Nike; I'm hoping they make him an offer."

"And how's my girl?"

"Leena? She's probably the happiest of all of us. Loving her job at the restaurant. Loving school. She's just a happy kid. Oh, and she's constantly bugging us to teach her to drive."

"So, the whole ordeal didn't have any kind of lasting impact on her?"

Callie was referring to Leena's kidnapping by Willow Weston and Hunter Tranton several months earlier.

"She talks about it all the time—like she's some Hollywood celebrity."

They both laughed.

"How's my wingman?" Deetz said, referring to Tyson, who'd been by his side in two harrowing, life-threatening situations.

"He's great. So happy to be back teaching. I think the time away from it really made him appreciate it."

"Wedding plans all good?"

"Oh my gosh, it's a lot." Callie chuckled. "But yeah, it's all good. We'll get there."

"That's going to be a festive celebration."

They made a bit more small talk and ended the call.

With the Willamette River now in view, Callie turned down Washington Avenue and headed the final stretch toward her high-rise. She glanced up and spotted her balcony, the one with the huge potted plant on the sixth floor.

She decided when she got up there she would make another cup of hot tea, do some research online, and make a few calls on

Sunny's behalf to find out the specifics on restraining orders and other options. Then she'd get some sleep before her night shift.

Her phone buzzed. She picked it up as she swung the VW into her parking deck. She activated her parking permit to lift the gate and pulled into the dark parking garage. With no cars behind her, she slowed and glanced at her phone.

It was a text from a number she didn't recognize: "Stay away from Sunny."

4

—————

THE HONK of a car horn echoed from behind and startled Callie. She'd been frozen, staring at the text message. She shot a look in the rearview mirror and saw a woman in a minivan holding her hands up in frustration. Callie tossed her phone in the passenger seat and drove up the ramp to the sixth floor of the parking deck.

The sickening feeling in her stomach took her right back to the frightening texts she used to receive from Keith Ramsey . . . "Where are you? Who are you with?"

No matter what answer she gave it was always the wrong one.

How dare Blaine Milligan find my number—and threaten me!

Even when she parked the Bug, walked to her entrance, scanned her ID, and opened the glass door to the long hallway leading to her sixth story apartment, Callie's face burned red hot with shock and anger—and fear.

She got inside, put her purse down, and stood there examining the text message again. "Stay away from Sunny."

Unbelievable!

Callie just couldn't fathom that a complete stranger had entered her personal space like that. She immediately texted Sunny and asked if the phone number from which the text had come was Blaine's. She stood there looking out at the gray sky and wide river in the distance, waiting for a response. But none came.

She turned on her electric tea kettle, kicked her shoes off, unplugged her laptop from the charger, and curled up on the end of the couch in the living room. First, she headed to her Facebook page to search Blaine Milligan. When she got to Facebook, she noticed a red dot up at the Friend Request icon. She clicked it to see who was reaching out.

The energy drained from her body.

Blaine Milligan.

The small round profile picture revealed a black and white caricature of a serious male face with exaggerated nose and ears.

Callie clicked his name to go to his page.

The large, horizontal cover photo showed a ravaged beach in what looked like the middle of a hurricane. Palm trees were bent sideways from excessive wind, branches and debris were strewn everywhere, enormous waves and whitecaps roared ashore. And there, standing in the midst of it all, to the far right side of the picture, was the silhouette of a man facing the ocean with his back to the camera, legs spread wide apart, hands stretched out to the gray sky.

Nutcase.

The tea kettle clicked off letting her know it was ready, but Callie was glued to the screen.

In the About section, it read:

- Worked at: "Name it. I've done it."
- Studied at: "School of Hard Knocks."
- Lives in: "Sunny Portland and wherever the wind blows."

Callie noted the play on the word Sunny and that he'd not mentioned being in a relationship. Interestingly, Callie and Blaine shared two mutual friends—Sunny and a guy named Trad Dupree, who Callie knew from her software programming classes at Seattle Central.

She scrolled down. It was obvious Blaine spent little time on the page. He had selected no interests. She clicked to look at his Friends. Besides Sunny and Trad, there were only about eight or nine, including scantily-dressed females of various ethnicities, and several sinister-looking dudes, one slouched way down in a big chair with a machine gun laying across his chest.

Callie scrolled through the sparse Timeline. The most recent entry was posted seven months earlier by one of Blaine's Friends,

Eddie Corbit. It showed Blaine wearing camo gear and a black ski cap, kneeling over a dead deer in a wet forest. The photo was taken with a flash at night or early morning. A rifle was strapped over Blaine's shoulder and he was staring at the camera with a stone cold sober scowl on his face. Eddie Corbit's words read: "The man finally gets himself a kill. Congrats Speed."

Callie wondered if "Speed" was Blaine Milligan's nickname. The way Deetz had described him, it would fit.

The few additional entries on the Timeline had been posted by other people. One was from a woman Callie assumed to be Blaine's sister. Her name was Bridget Reedy. The entry simply read: "Happy Birthday." The old photo was of a little girl with her arm around a little boy. Probably them, as children, standing in a kitchen.

She clicked his Photos next and was immediately creeped out. There were only three pictures. Each one, it appeared, Blaine Milligan had taken of himself. Dark, mysterious head-and-shoulders shots, each at a weird angle and somewhat blurred. She expanded one of the photos. It gave her chills. He was not a handsome man. Dark hair cut high up on his large forehead. Noticeable crevice between his deep-set, steely eyes. She clicked to the next picture. Long, knobby nose. Small mouth with a tiny, almost nonexistent mustache. He looked drunk. She clicked to the last photo. Long, floppy ears. Sideburns. Rugged, narrow face with indents below high cheek bones. Elongated jaw. Thick neck. Protruding Adam's apple.

Callie searched around a bit more, finding it odd the only mention Blaine had made of Sunny was in his comment about living in "Sunny Portland." That was it.

Out of curiosity, Callie clicked on Sunny's Facebook page. She didn't recall looking at it in any detail when they'd become Friends. Of course, she didn't know then what she knew now about Blaine Milligan.

Sunny's cover shot was a horizontal photo of her pretty little yellow house at dusk with stark shadows and vivid colors. Unlike Blaine's profile, Sunny's stated she was in a relationship. And her photos showed three or four shots of she and Blaine. He'd taken most of the pictures—selfies. Most were in bars or dark restaurants, and Sunny looked peculiarly out of it in each of them.

The whole thing gave Callie a sick feeling deep in the pit of her stomach, especially knowing this weirdo had actually texted her—and sent a Friend request.

Gross.

Her phone buzzed nearby somewhere, but she didn't see it. She looked at her Apple watch. It was Sunny calling. She quickly got up and tossed the pillows away, then removed the cushion she'd been sitting on.

The phone was there. She grabbed it.

"Sunny?"

"Hey, that is Blaine's number. What's going on?" Sunny said, out of breath. "He didn't call you . . ."

Callie thought about how to respond as she crossed to the sliding glass door, opened it and stepped out on to the balcony. "He texted me."

"What?" She gasped. "What did he say?"

"Stay away from Sunny."

"Oh my gosh. Oh my gosh . . . He did not. He did not . . ."

"Sunny, you need to tell me what's going on? Is Blaine threatening you? Is he hurting you? I told you—"

"This is not good. This is so *not* good. Oh dear, Callie, why did you bring your cop friend here?" Sunny shouted. "He was here when Blaine got here. They had words! Blaine took off. He called me. I've never heard him so ticked off."

"Sunny, I've told you about the Dorcas House . . ."

"You need to block his number and tell your friend Deetz to watch his back. You need to keep your doors locked."

"Sunny, he also sent me a Friend request—on Facebook."

Silence.

She could hear Sunny walking fast, breathing hard.

"We need to talk, in person," Callie said.

"Are you kidding me? That's the *last* thing we need. He's on to you. This is not good. I need to see him. I just need to get with him and defuse it. That's what I'm doing. I'm shopping now, gonna make his favorite dinner, dessert—"

"Sunny, it's obvious what's happening. I've told you, I've been through this. I see the signs. I hear it in your voice."

"Leave me alone, Callie. Okay? No one understands this."

"I do understand. I've—"

"No one knows Blaine Milligan, okay?"

"I had my nose broken, Sunny. Ribs broken."

"And you went to that shelter and your man didn't find you. He was *not* Blaine Milligan. He would find me. It's a fact, it's not a question."

"Can we just meet? I just want you to tell me, in person, what's going on and then I can help you take the next steps." Callie was thinking if they met in person she might be able to take her straight to the shelter.

"Excuse me . . . I was in this line first." Sunny was talking to someone else. "I've got to go, Callie."

"Sunny, please, let's meet. I'll be available wherever, whenever you say. It can be a secret."

"Ha. See! You haven't been through what I have—at all. In my world, there are no secrets, Callie. He's watching. Always. Twenty-four seven."

"That's precisely why you need to get out."

"Of my own house? Look, you've been a good friend, Callie, but I think we need to take a break. When this cools off, I'll reach back out."

"No you won't."

"I've got to pay. I'm in line. Good bye, Callie. Thanks for trying."

The line went dead.

5

Deetz sat dumbfounded in the swivel chair in his cubicle at Portland Police headquarters. He was bent over with his elbows on his knees and his head down, reflecting on the meeting he'd just come from in the conference room down the hall. And thinking about the police body cam footage he'd watched probably a half-dozen times.

In the meeting, Sergeant Tidwell updated Deetz and the team on Portland PD officer Wiley Fleming, who was in jail, awaiting charges for killing a twenty-seven-year-old Black man, Ronald Jacoby, days earlier. Jacoby and a friend were driving through the city in an old Chevy Impala when officer Fleming, a Caucasian, pulled them over for a burned-out taillight.

According to officer Fleming—and his body cam footage, and videos shot by bystanders—Jacoby got out of his car without being asked. When officer Fleming directed Jacoby to get back in the Impala, he refused and, instead, began walking straight toward officer Fleming in a combative and disorderly manner.

As Jacoby got closer, officer Fleming gave verbal warning and drew his standard-issued 9mm Glock 17 handgun. "What are you gonna do, shoot me?" Jacoby taunted.

With the Glock pointed directly at Jacoby's chest, officer Fleming ordered the man to stand down. But he would not. Sergeant Tidwell informed the group in the meeting that, according to toxicology reports, Jacoby's blood alcohol level was .14, almost double the legal limit.

When Jacoby got within two feet of Fleming, he suddenly changed his tune, insisting he had been kidding, and kindly asked what the officer had pulled him over for. When officer Fleming began to holster his weapon, Jacoby darted for the gun. A fight ensued as the two men intertwined and dropped to the pavement in a wrestling match for the weapon.

One of the first rules police officers are taught in firearms training is—*never* allow your weapon to be taken.

There was a gun blast.

Ronald Jacoby was dead within forty-five seconds.

Since then, Portland's streets had been filled with unrest and protestors, especially at night, to the point where Mayor Barbara Meeks announced an eight o'clock curfew. Amidst the marches and demands to defund the police, there was major looting, rioting, and mayhem.

Deetz sat quietly in deep thought.

He remembered the law enforcement code of ethics he'd sworn to long ago—to safeguard lives and property; to protect the innocent against deception, the weak against oppression or intimidation, and the peaceful against violence and disorder. He'd always tried to do that, regardless of a person's skin color.

Deetz knew there were prejudiced cops and those who abused their power. People were sick and tired of it. He got that. He wanted them weeded out, too. And he saw the need for reform. But to vilify all police officers, the majority of whom were in the job to serve the community and safeguard lives and property? The people in the meeting from which he'd just come, for instance, his colleagues, were darn good people. After all these years on the force, most of them were like family to Deetz—Sergeant Tidwell, Investigator Virgil Bennett, Detectives Angie Cook, Wesley Fitch, and Ben Briggs.

Yet, mobs were out there literally destroying the beautiful downtown area, firebombing cars, smashing windows, and stealing from local businesses—it infuriated Deetz.

It made him want to quit. Be done with it. He had that option. He'd thought about it so much it was making him lose sleep.

Cops had enough pressure, arriving at real-time crime situations that were dicey and dangerous. And now, instead of reacting instantly and instinctively, they would be second-guessing their every step—and possibly getting gunned down in the process.

Joanie had pleaded with Deetz to retire early, to just quit. She wanted him safe and healthy so they could sail into the sunset in good health; that was all that mattered to her. But he would lose a huge chunk of his pension if he did that, and he couldn't pull the trigger on that one. He was determined to stick it out another year—or, four hundred fourteen days, to be exact.

He paused and chuckled to himself at the irony of his stage of life. He remembered growing up, hearing the older generation complain about the younger "hippie" generation—calling them a bunch of "lazy, pot-smoking, peace-loving, flower children." And now he was the grouchy old man, thinking the younger generation were a bunch of spoiled brats who'd been brought up by helicopter parents, getting trophies for participation and forcing their beliefs on everyone.

He thought of J.P. and Brandon, how someday they'd be raising kids in a different world than he grew up in. It would be much more difficult for them to impart Christian values to their kids in a society that was forcing *everything* to be acceptable—even if God disapproved of it; and where political correctness took precedence over Biblical truth.

His phone vibrated, snapping him back to reality.

It was Callie.

"Now what?" he answered in jest.

"You're not gonna believe it, Wayne." In a hurried tone, she filled Deetz in on the threatening text she received from Blaine Milligan, and the Friend request. "Sunny basically admitted he's nuts," Callie said. "She told me to tell you to watch your back. She told me to keep my doors locked! I told her again about the Dorcas House, but she honestly doesn't believe she can escape him. It's like he's got complete control."

"I need to look into this guy," Deetz said, swiveling to his desk and waking up his computer. "I'll run him through our database."

"Let me know, okay?"

"Of course. Have you told Tyson about all this?"

"Not yet. I'm going to text him and have him call me. You're not concerned, are you? For my safety or anything?"

"No . . . but, it is pretty bold—to do what he did. He's a loose cannon, for sure. Let me see what I can find out. But I know that to get a restraining order Sunny's going to have to file a police report."

"I'm going to research all that now."

"Thanks for keeping me up to date. Has he been back to Sunny's?"

"No. And she was out shopping, getting stuff to make his favorite dinner, if you can believe that. I honestly think she's being brainwashed."

"Let me see what I can find out."

They ended the call.

Deetz stood and stretched. He'd done nothing but sit all morning.

He bent down and got his beloved silver thermos, which Joanie faithfully filled each morning with double-strong coffee. He poured a cup, took a seat, and fired up the database to see if there were any bones in Blaine Milligan's closet.

His phone buzzed. It was a text from Joanie: "I know you're in a meeting. Call me when done. Something weird just happened."

6

Sunny let out an audible sigh of relief when she saw Blaine's truck was not in the driveway at her house. She zipped her little Ford Focus into the garage and closed the garage door.

As she set the groceries on the counter in the kitchen, she tried to ignore her racing heart. She stared down at her trembling hands. *This is not normal.* She gripped the counter with both hands as if trying to keep her balance on a ship in a storm.

Look what he's doing to you.

She'd turned her phone off because she feared Blaine's repeated calls and texts were going to give her a nervous breakdown. She knew she would pay for it later. But she also knew she would be the object of his wrath anyway, so why not try to find a little relief in the meantime?

There was a small chance she could win him over by pampering him. She doubted it would work because of what had happened that morning with the Portland PD guy, Deetz. But she had to try.

She quickly put the six-pack of RedBull, his favorite drink, in the fridge and got out the ingredients she needed to make the marinade for the flank steak. She filled the glass baking dish with Italian dressing, soy sauce, lemon juice, ginger, white wine, and Worcestershire sauce, then set the big steak in and shook on some salt, pepper, and capers.

She washed the potatoes and, as she began making the salad,

the same old queasiness returned to her stomach as she replayed the morning events in her mind—telling Callie she couldn't go shopping, meeting Deetz, then literally biting her bottom lip as she watched Blaine jump out of his truck like a lunatic to confront Deetz.

She looked at the time. She should be having lunch with Callie, surrounded by shopping bags and looking forward to a fun afternoon. Instead, she was home on her day off enacting a battle plan in an attempt to fend off Blaine's fury. Her body was still sore and bruised from the last time. She began to replay it—the belt cracking her legs and back, her scrambling under the bed, him pulling her out by an ankle.

She was wobbly . . . weak.

Nauseous.

She steadied herself at the sink. Turned on the water. Drank from her hand. Splashed her face. Let it drip. Determined to block it out. Block it out. Block it out.

She stared into the small backyard.

You are so messed up. You're making dinner for the man who beats you to a pulp.

The grass in back was high. Of course, Blaine never mowed or did anything like that. She did all the upkeep. He just came and went as he pleased.

When he was there, he was one hundred percent there and they were supposed to be the happy, all-American couple. A very small percentage of the time, they were. But she could never completely let her guard down. To some extent, she always walked on eggshells.

When Blaine was gone, which he could be for days, she didn't hear from him much—but she knew he was watching, either driving by periodically or keeping track of her on the Find My Friends app; which he insisted she keep turned on at all times. She'd learned her lesson on that.

Over the months Sunny had come to sum it up this way in her mind: Blaine was obsessed with controlling her. That was the most important thing in his life.

How did I get here? How did I let this happen?

I used to be free. The future was so bright. I worked my buns off to get my degree and a good job with the city. I bought a new car and my own house. I'm a strong woman . . .

But the dreaded night she met Blaine at The Peacock, an underground bar in downtown Portland, her life was altered, forever. If she could change one thing in her life, it would be that night. She would never have gone to that bar and, therefore, never would have met Blaine Milligan.

Oh, if only . . . I would be free now.

The water was still running. She turned it off, snatched a towel, patted her face, and dried her hands.

She'd had too much to drink that night at The Peacock and let him persuade her into going back to her house.

That was it.

The lid to Pandora's box had been bashed open.

She'd let a reprobate saunter into her world.

From that night onward, the life she'd once known had vanished.

She was his now. In fact, she could barely remember what it had been like "BB," an expression she used for, "Before Blaine."

He'd actually been charming at first, for a few days.

But she would never forget the first shocking jolt she'd taken from him. She'd never been hit before, by anyone. It literally shook her brain and her cheek burned, then turned numb for hours.

They'd been sitting at a table for two outside of a small eatery in the city, having a drink and a good time getting to know each other. She caught a glimpse of a man crossing the street, an older guy, handsome. She'd thought of it a million times since then. Had she done anything wrong? She hadn't even realized she was looking at the man.

And, *boom.*

Her lights went out.

From nowhere, Blaine bashed her face with the back of his beefy hand. It practically knocked her out of her chair. She saw stars. She was dazed and in shock. He looked around to make sure no one had seen, then leaned close to her, propped her up, and gave that evil smile. "What are you looking at, Sunny? You're with me now. You don't look at other men. Never again. Okay?"

Standing there in the kitchen, Sunny realized tears had flooded her eyes. She grabbed the towel and wiped them, mad at herself for remembering. She got back to tearing the lettuce, making the salad, rehearsing what she would say when he arrived. All she could think up was a far-fetched lie—that Callie had forgotten her umbrella at the Deetz's house, and he was dropping it off to her at Sunny's place on his way to work. It was a real stretch, but it was all she had.

Her mind kept pushing her back to that first time, that first . . . beating. It was almost like God or some higher power was forcing her to remember now—to face the truth about how she was living, about the predicament she was in.

When they'd returned home from the eatery that day, back to her house, Blaine apologized. He didn't get emotional or anything, like he had several times since then, but he simply said something like, "I'm sorry about what happened. It just made me jealous to see you looking at another man. I want to be all yours and I want to be the only one you ever think of."

Sunny had been so numb from the strike that, even though she'd found Blaine attractive and fun to be with those first few days, she was not going to see him again. She'd heard about guys like him. Control freaks. Abusers. Strike now, apologize later. She would have no part of it. She would stop it cold. She would end it before it began.

At least, that had been the plan.

She staggered back against the kitchen cupboards as she remembered Blaine showing up at the house that night. Even though Sunny had lied to him over the phone saying she'd had a headache and didn't want to do anything—he'd showed up at the front door. When she lied to him again, through the door, saying she had a migraine, he left in a huff.

She thought he'd left.

But within about fifteen minutes . . . she smelled cigar smoke.

She crossed to the back of the house, quietly opened the door and tiptoed a few steps out. The smell got stronger.

Blaine's truck was still in the driveway. It was turned off and dark inside, but smoke drifted out the driver's window.

She remembered vividly that it had crossed her mind that instant to call the police. But knowing the Blaine she knew now, she realized, it wouldn't have mattered if she had called them. He'd picked her. And there was no stopping him from owning her.

She'd crept back into the house and made sure the doors were locked.

Minutes later she heard a loud rattle at the front door. She would never, ever forget that sound.

Because, then, the front door flew open and Blaine Milligan took a giant step into her world.

And he was smiling that evil smile.

And shaking his big head.

And holding up a key he'd had made that afternoon.

7

Callie texted Tyson and asked him to call her when he had a
break at school. Then she called the city's Domestic Violence Division and introduced herself to an employee named Ann Pierce. "I
have a girlfriend who I think is being abused by her boyfriend,"
Callie said. "I just need to know what her options are as far as
getting help . . . protection?"

"Our office can help once she files a police report against the
man," Ann said. "When she does that, someone from the district
attorney's office will be appointed to assist her in the court process,
with a restraining order or whatever. Then the district attorney
would decide if formal charges would be filed and an arrest made."

"What if she's not ready to press charges?" Callie said.

"You or another person could file the police report, if you
witnessed the abuse. Otherwise, our office can't help. Someone has
to file a police report for us to get involved. However, if there's an
emergency she can contact the Women's Crisis Hotline or Call for
Shelter. There are also domestic violence shelters in the city. I can
give you—"

"I know about those."

"She should also have a well thought out Safety Plan in place,"
Ann said. "It's kind of like an escape plan. You can find guidance for
that on our website."

"I'm on there now. Where exactly?" Callie said.

"Left column, down toward the bottom. You can download a PDF of the brochure."

Callie clicked it on and sent it to her printer.

Ann said, "Since you're a close friend, you can be watching for unusual behavior, bruises, emotional distress."

"I've seen all that, that's why I'm calling."

"Has your friend confided in you directly that she's being abused?" Ann said.

Callie paused. "Not yet, but I know she is. I was abused. I know the signs."

"You really shouldn't confront her about it. It's important for her to self-disclose. You can express concern, be willing to listen, be supportive. When she's ready, she'll confide in you. In the meantime, you can become as familiar as possible with all the resources available from local government. When she does confide in you, you can make sure she develops a thorough Safety Plan."

Callie ended the call frustrated, not with the Domestic Violence Division, but with Sunny—for not filing a police report, for not getting the heck out of there.

She went into her bedroom, grabbed the printout and began reading on her way back to the couch.

- When the abuser is there and an argument ensues, stay out of rooms with no exits (bathrooms) and rooms with weapons (kitchen)

- Think about what you will say to your partner if he/she becomes violent

- Make a list of people to contact

- Establish a code word or phrase that alerts friends or family to call the police

- Have a suitcase packed and ready to go with the following items:

Photo ID
Birth certificate
Social Security Card
Passport
Marriage certificate
Money, ATM/credit cards, check books, bank books

Lease, rental agreement, deed
Car registration, proof of insurance
Keys to residence
Toiletries
Clothes
Documentation of past abuse: photos, journal, medical
records, police reports

Callie turned the tea kettle back on in the kitchen, then plopped down on the couch in the family room and continued reading the brochure's instructions for if/when the abuser moved out. Those included everything from changing locks on the doors and windows to installing peepholes, changing phone numbers, increasing outdoor lighting, and getting a dog; she assumed they meant a large, mean dog.

Even though Ann Pierce had advised Callie not to confront Sunny directly, she was determined to help her be ready to leave in a flash if and when the need arose. She arranged the printout of the Safety Plan-packing list on the table, took a picture of it, and texted it to Sunny without further explanation. Callie could never forgive herself if she didn't do all in her power to help Sunny. Now, she could only hope Sunny would heed the advice and secretly get prepared to make a fast exit.

On her laptop, Callie visited the Call for Shelter website, which she'd visited in the past when Keith Ramsey was still alive. It provided information about the four domestic violence shelters in and around Portland. Nothing much she didn't already know.

At the Women's Crisis Hotline website it described domestic violence as "an ongoing pattern of hurtful, manipulative or controlling activities that result in one partner or spouse being afraid of the other."

Her phone rang. Tyson's photo popped up. She answered.

"Hey, Cooper. Thanks for calling back."

"Hey, Freeland, what's going on? Everything okay?"

"Eh. Something happened I want to tell you about. It kind of freaked me out a little bit."

"What?"

"You know I was going to get Sunny and go for coffee and shopping?"

"Right."

"When I got there she said she couldn't go."

"Okay . . ."

"She said Blaine was upset about something and was on his way home, so she couldn't go."

"This is the guy you suspect might be abusing her?"

"Right. So, on a whim I called Wayne thinking he could stop by if he was on his way in to work."

"Callie, no you didn't."

"Yeah. He was fine with it. I met him out front."

"If this guy is as crazy as you think he is, that probably wasn't a good idea."

Callie swallowed hard and her mind raced. She shouldn't have called Tyson. She should have just waited till they were together to explain everything.

"Are you in a hurry?" she asked.

"I mean, I don't have much time. But now you have me. What happened?"

"I introduced Wayne to Sunny out front, then I left."

"Okay . . ."

"But Wayne was there when Blaine came home."

"What did you get Wayne into, Freeland?"

"It's like I've said all along, Cooper, this Blaine guy's a nutcase. He threatened Wayne. They had words. He took off." She did not want to tell him about the text message and Facebook request. He was *not* going to be happy.

Knock, knock, knock.

Someone was at the door.

Callie stood.

Tyson was saying something, but she was distracted.

"Hold on, hon, someone's at the door," Callie said on her way to answer.

"Okay, look, I need to get back. You want to finish telling me later?"

"Well, yeah, I haven't got to the worst part yet, though," Callie said, holding her breath as she made her way to the door.

"What do you mean? Tell me. What happened?"

"I got a text message from him saying to stay away from Sunny."

There. She was relieved to have gotten that part out.

Tyson was instantly agitated. "How did he get your number?"

"I have no idea."

"What did the text message say, exactly?"

She told him again.

"Forward it to me, will you, please?"

"Okay, hold on." Callie got to the door, put him on speaker, and forwarded him the text from Blaine. "Okay, done." She peered through the peephole and saw no one in the hallway. But something was sitting on the floor outside the door, something red. She couldn't make out what it was.

Tyson started to ask her questions to which she didn't know the answers.

"Stop Cooper. I'm not done." She was determined to forge ahead. "He also sent me a Friend Request on Facebook."

"What?" He was ticked, now. "What's this guy's full name and where does he live?"

Tyson didn't get angry often, but when he did, he could go really ballistic.

Callie opened the door and her senses were instantly assaulted by the overpowering smell of gasoline.

She looked down and froze.

Tyson was talking but she didn't hear what he was saying.

At her feet in the condo hallway was a large puddle of gasoline and splashes of it against her door and walls. In the middle of the puddle sat a brand new, red gas can with a large spout. In black marker on the side of the can it read: *Next time I light it.*

8

———

Deetz took the lunch and bottled water he'd packed to the break room at Portland PD headquarters and found a high-top seat by a window. The afternoon sun peeked through the rolling clouds, then hid itself. He got the lunch spread out, took a bite of his roast beef sandwich, and called Joanie.

"What weird thing just happened?" he said.

She laughed. "How was the meeting?"

"Depressing. The morale around here is in the tank."

"I can imagine. I just heard on the news they think that cop Fleming is going to get felony murder charges and aggravated assault with a deadly weapon."

"Yeah, we're hearing that, too."

"You could be done with it all, Wayne. Why take the chance—"

"Honey, honey," he interrupted. "What weird thing just happened?"

"Yeah, yeah, change the subject, like always."

"Yep." He continued eating.

"You know how I throw things away all the time, by accident?"

"Uh oh."

She giggled. "Remember me telling you my car tag sticker thingy came in the mail?"

"Uh oh." He laughed.

"I thought I'd thrown it away by accident. I was sure I did.

Because, when my registration came in the mail, I didn't see the sticker in there with it and I couldn't find it anywhere. So I got online and found out there's a little pocket on the inside of the envelope where they put the sticker. A lot of people throw it away, I found out."

"Sure, sure. So, what happened? The suspense is killing me."

"Are you eating?"

"Yeah. Why?"

"I can hear you chewing."

"Oh . . . well that's what you do when you eat, dear."

"So anyway, I ran out to the big garbage can at the curb, because the trash guys were due to come, and I opened it to get the last bag of trash and guess what?"

"You fell in?" He chuckled.

"Very funny. No. The trash bag wasn't there."

Deetz stopped chewing and the image of Blaine Milligan ripped through his mind.

"In fact," Joanie continued, "it looked like more than one bag was gone. Did you move them or something?"

"Did you see any cars or trucks along the street? Anyone unusual hanging around?" Deetz folded up the remainder of his lunch.

"No . . ."

"A big white pickup?"

"Why a white pickup? You're scaring me, Wayne."

He stood and looked out the window. "I had an incident this morning. Callie called me."

"You told me you were stopping at her friend's place."

"That's right. I did. I met her friend—Sunny. Callie left and I was leaving too, but then Sunny's boyfriend came home—the one Callie thinks is beating up on her."

"And . . ."

"We had a confrontation."

"Oh no, Wayne. Say you didn't."

"It wasn't my fault, honey. I was just sitting in my car. He got all over me. Threatened me—and Callie."

"Here we go again."

"I may be wrong. I hope I am."

"What would he want with our trash?"

"Who knows? But I need to check the credit cards and make sure he hasn't tapped into them."

"But you shred everything."

"Um. I've been getting lazy with that." In fact, he hadn't been doing it. "Anything else unusual around the house? Can you look out front real quick, make sure his truck's not there?"

Deetz could hear Joanie moving. He hated to scare her. This would only add to her beef with this job.

"What went on in this exchange that would make this guy come here, Wayne? What'd you do?"

"Nothing honey!"

"Did you antagonize him?"

"No! I think he has mental issues. He's bipolar."

"Darn it, Wayne. We get out of one fire and we're right back into another."

"Tell me what you see out front."

"Nothing."

"Okay, I'm gonna check the credit cards, then I need to look into this guy's background. Don't worry, babe. The chances are slim this guy did this. Anyone could have gotten into the trash."

"What's his name?" Joanie said.

"Why?"

"I'm gonna check him out online."

He hesitated. "Blaine Milligan."

"Okay, bye. I'm taking Leena to the dentist."

"Oh, right. Thanks for doing that," Deetz said. "Hey, keep the garage door down and the doors locked . . . just in case."

"The day you quit this job will be the happiest day of my life."

DEETZ THREW the remainder of his lunch in the trash and headed to his cubicle, replaying the disquieting exchange with Blaine Milligan from that morning.

During his thirty-four years on the force, he'd dealt with a lot of unstable, dangerous people, but rarely did those encounters become personal. It nagged at him in an unsettling way that Blaine

Milligan had said, "You're in my world now," and had threatened Callie and him.

He took a seat, fired up his laptop, and logged into his main credit card company. After tapping around he found the latest charges and determined there had been no unusual recent activity.

Good.

Next, he checked their secondary credit card and found nothing unusual there, either.

Relieved, he closed the laptop, rolled over and logged onto his desktop computer, and entered Oregon's police database, LEDS—the Law Enforcement Data Systems. He typed in Blaine Milligan. After a moment, several mugshots of Milligan appeared, and a list dropped down of at least a dozen charges and offenses.

Deetz felt his face flush.

He leaned closer and began reading. There were charges of various crimes against persons, three simple assaults, theft from auto, several trespassing charges, and one count of larceny.

Deetz glanced up at the latest of Milligan's mugshots, at his narrow, crazy eyes, large nose, sucked-in cheeks, sinister scowl. His shirt collar was torn, his dark hair was a mess, and he had a deep gash along his rigid jaw. Date of birth 1984, which made him thirty-six. Never married.

Deetz went back to the rap sheet. Milligan had been convicted of misdemeanor charges including harassment, menacing, and strangulation. Callie's worst suspicions and fears were right there in writing. Rivulets of sweat broke out on Deetz's forehead. It appeared the charges were filed by a number of different women, none being Sunny.

As Deetz continued down the list—criminal mischief, methamphetamine possession, and restraining order violations—he realized the whole situation may've just shifted from a personal matter to a police matter.

Milligan had been convicted of most of the crimes for which he was charged and had served about three years, on and off, at both the Oregon State Penitentiary in Salem and the Columbia River Correctional Institution in Portland. That was all before 2007.

His big downfall came several years later when he was charged with and convicted of arson, a boat fire with serious injuries. He fled unlawfully to avoid prosecution and was tracked down in Mt. Hood National Forest. For those crimes he served an additional four-and-a-half years at Clackamas County Jail in Oregon City.

Deetz worked the mouse, clicked, and found Milligan's most current address—south of the city in Oatfield, and his most current occupation—lumber yard associate.

Deetz sent all the information to the printer and dropped back in his chair, stretched, and clasped his hands behind his head. His whole body was stiff. He closed his eyes, took several deep breaths, tried to relax.

Blaine Milligan was trouble. Deetz wondered if he'd returned to Sunny's house yet, and if so, what price she may have had to pay for Callie and Deetz showing up there that morning?

He looked at his watch. It was approaching 2 p.m. During the next few hours he would contemplate stopping back at Sunny's on his way home from work. He didn't want to, but for her well-being, he thought he probably should. If they were both there, that would be best. He could confront the situation with both of them. Let them know he's aware of Milligan's rap sheet. Issue a warning that if anything happens to her, he will be arrested.

"Wayne, buddy, can I borrow you for a few?" Long-time colleague and friend Virgil Bennett smacked the wall of Deetz's cubicle.

"What's up?" Deetz said.

"We got protestors out front. It's growing fast." Virgil drummed the top of the cubicle. "We're rounding up as many bodies as we can downstairs. Sarge has them getting on riot gear in the staging area. He wants me to refresh them on riot control tactics before they go out, and he wants you and Fitch there too, to help answer questions and deploy."

Deetz stood. "Let me take a look outside before we hit the staging area."

"Ten-four. Fitch is meeting us at the front doors right now."

9
____

Tyson Cooper had quickly ended the call with Callie, hurried to the principal's office, told Mrs. Melvin the long-time receptionist he had an emergency, and got uptown to Callie's place as fast as he could. By the time he fought city traffic, found a place to park, and got to the sixth floor, it was mid-afternoon. He rang the bell at the security door to let Callie know he was there. She buzzed him in.

He was immediately hit with the strong smell of fuel as he hurried down the long breezeway, stepped around the puddle of what he presumed was gas, and knocked. The gas was still wet low on the walls outside Callie's door, just as she'd described.

The door unlocked. He pushed it open. Callie was walking away from him like a zombie toward the balcony. She had on jeans and a sweatshirt. Her sandy colored hair was pulled back beneath a white headband.

Tyson immediately saw the red gas can on the floor, and the ominous black message: *Next time I light it.* He ignored it and tried to control his rage as he followed her out to the balcony. His heart was pounding.

"Hey, Freeland. Hey, pal." From behind he rested his hands atop her shoulders and fought to keep his trembling voice calm. "It's okay. I'm here. I'm here, okay?"

She nodded. "Thanks for coming, Cooper. You didn't have to leave school."

He stepped in front of her, bent down, and looked into her brown eyes. "I'm sorry this happened, but I'm here now, okay? You don't have to worry. I'll take care of this. Wayne will help us."

She reached up and squeezed his arms. "I can't believe anyone would do this."

Tyson looked back at the gas can. "I know. I know. It'll be okay."

She stepped closer and hugged him.

He put his arms around her and held her.

"How do you think he got in here?" Tyson said.

"Probably followed a neighbor in. It's not hard."

"I called Deetz on the way over. Got his voicemail," Tyson said.

"Did you leave a message?"

"Yeah."

"I need to call Sunny," Callie said.

"Not now, okay?" Tyson said. "Let's see what Deetz wants to do."

"I need to convince her to get out of there," Callie said.

"You really think it would be wise to contact Sunny in any way, shape, or form right now?"

She backed away and crossed her arms. "I'm cold." She walked back inside, and he followed. She yanked the sliding glass door closed.

"It smells," she said, walking to the kitchen.

"The police will need to see the can. I'll put it out on the balcony till Wayne gets here." Tyson grabbed a paper towel from the kitchen, crossed to the gas can, and picked it up using the paper towel so he didn't get his fingerprints on it. Gasoline sloshed around in the bottom.

"I picked it up with my hands," Callie said. "I wasn't thinking."

"That's okay. We'll tell them." He set it on the balcony and came back inside.

"Will you show me the Friend Request?" Tyson said.

"You can look." She pointed to her laptop on the coffee table. "It's probably still on there. You want something to drink or anything?"

"I'm good. Thanks." He grabbed the laptop, sat in the chair near the balcony, and opened it. Callie's Facebook page came up. He found the Friend Request and clicked onto Blaine Milligan's Facebook page. He was immediately struck by the brash, rugged look of the man.

"Find it?" she called.

"Yeah."

"I'm making tea. Want some?"

"No. Did you block his number from your phone?"

"Yes."

With a feeling of numbness and quiet outrage, Tyson examined Blaine Milligan's bio, his photos, and the few posts available. The wheels in Tyson's head were turning about what would happen next. He wished Deetz would call.

"I can't get warm." Holding a cup of hot tea in both hands, Callie crossed to the thermostat and Tyson heard the heat kick on.

She then walked over and curled up on the couch.

Tyson picked up the laptop and moved over to sit next to her.

"I don't want to see that anymore," she said.

"Okay." He closed the computer, set it on the table in front of the couch, and dropped back next to her.

"You're supposed to work tonight, aren't you?" he said.

"Yeah."

"You think maybe you should take the night off?"

"Can't stop living," she said.

"Maybe you should pack a bag and hang out at my place for a few days."

She pursed her lips and rocked her head back and forth, thinking about it. "I don't know."

"Just to be safe," he said.

"I have my stun gun." She got up, scooted into the kitchen, and began digging through a drawer.

"Seriously?" Tyson said. "That little thing?"

She held it up. It was about the size of a deck of cards. "It needs a charge." She plugged it into the wall outlet above the counter. "This is the kind you need to make contact with their body. It doesn't shoot anything out, so you need to zap them up close."

Tyson nodded, going along with it, glad she hadn't lost her sense of humor. What was really needed in this situation was a gun, he thought. Ever since his wife Kim had been murdered in the Portland massacre of 2018, he carried a Sig Sauer P226 .40 caliber pistol strapped to his ankle whenever possible. He shifted his leg and felt the weight of it. If it hadn't been for that weapon, many people would have died at the one-year anniversary of the Portland attack, when he ended up gunning down a copycat shooter.

In Oregon, individual school districts implemented their own gun policies. His school did not permit teachers to carry. So, the gun remained in his car on school days. He'd put it on before coming in.

Two loud knocks at the door.

"Oh my gosh," Callie jumped back, hand to her chest.

Tyson was up in an instant and at the door, about to draw the weapon. He peered through the peephole and saw a woman's face, her forehead and brown glasses magnified almost comically through the viewing device.

"Who is it?" Callie said.

"Some lady. Come here."

Callie went to the door and looked through the peephole. "My neighbor, from down the hall." She pulled the door open.

"Hey." Jeannie gave a hesitant wave to Callie and made an exaggerated leap around what was left of the gasoline. "I'm Jeannie from sixty-two-ten. We met at the Christmas party last year."

"I remember." Callie nodded. "This is my friend, Tyson."

They acknowledged each other.

"What's going on . . . with the gas?" Jeannie said.

"We're not sure," Tyson spoke up.

"You might want to sweep away what's left of this puddle, you know, just to be safe," Jeannie said.

Tyson and Callie both nodded. "Good idea. I'll do that," Tyson said.

Jeannie looked past them, into Callie's apartment. "I did see a man with a gas can."

"Please, come in." Tyson stepped aside and extended a hand.

"Not necessary. I just—"

"Can you tell us what you saw, exactly?" Tyson said.

"I was coming in from my car. Had my arms full of groceries. Managed to swipe my card. And, from out of nowhere this man grabs the door from behind, opens it for me. 'Go ahead,' he says. He was carrying a red gas can." She looked past them again, craning her neck, her eyes darting about the condo. "He acted like he lived here. Barged right in. Asked if I needed any more help. I said no."

"Then what?" Callie said.

"I kept going down the hall to my place. The last I saw, he was looking back and forth at the numbers. He saw me looking back at him and he said, 'Be on your way.' Can you believe that? I went in, of course; wasn't going to stand around out here and get mugged. So, what'd he do? What's going on? Do I need to call the police?"

"Are you sure you won't come in?" Tyson said.

"Yes. I'm afraid he's going to burn this place down."

"We've contacted the police," Tyson said. "Someone, probably the man you described, splashed gas outside Callie's door and left a threatening message. She doesn't know this man. Can you describe him?"

"Big, huge guy. Just an overpowering aura about him. Confident. Serious face. Not attractive. Smelled good. Dark brown-gray hair, not long."

Tyson looked at Callie. "Will you get your laptop, show her a photo?"

Without a word, Callie went to get her computer. She came back with it open to Blaine Milligan's Facebook page, and to one of the clearer photos of him.

"That's him," Jeannie said. "So you *do* know him."

Tyson could tell she was scanning the screen for his name and he signaled for Callie to close the laptop, which she did.

"We don't know him. We suspect this is him," Tyson said.

"So, the police are on the way?" Jeannie said.

"I've contacted them, yes," Tyson said.

"What did the message say—that he left?" Jeannie said.

Tyson glanced at Callie. "We're going to leave that to the police."

"If he threatened to start a fire, I have a right to know; all the residents do." Jeannie stared at Tyson, then Callie.

"We're as concerned as you are, Jeannie," said Callie.

"We're going to do exactly what the police tell us to do," Tyson said. "If they feel it's necessary to warn residents, I'm sure they'll do that."

"All right." Jeannie backed up and took another exaggerated step around the diminishing puddle of fuel. "Do you have a mop? To sweep this up?"

"Yes," Callie said. "I'll take care of that. Thank you for coming over."

"I wouldn't want someone to drop a cigarette, you know —kablooey."

"Jeannie," Tyson said. "You didn't happen to see him in the parking deck and notice his car?"

"No, no, nope. Just when he followed me in."

They said their goodbyes.

Callie and Tyson rounded up a mop, some rags, a bucket of water, and some other cleaning supplies and got busy cleaning up the gas from the breezeway.

"I want you to live at my house for now. Will you do that?" he said.

"Man, Cooper, this really has you freaked out," Callie said.

"Freeland, this is *not* normal behavior. This is dangerous."

"I know! But I don't want to let some loser dictate the way I live my life," Callie said. "I mean, I'm not saying no, and I appreciate the offer. But it just ticks me off."

"It'll just be for a few days. Look, if he has the audacity to do this . . . you need to play it on the safe side."

"You've been looking for an excuse like this, to get me to stay over," she joked.

"Oh right. You work all night. We won't even be there at the same time."

"I was kidding, Cooper. Calm down."

He stopped cleaning.

He reached out, squeezed her arm, and looked deep into her eyes. "I love you, Freeland. I don't want to take any chances." After all, he'd already lost one wife.

She smiled and gave him a quick kiss.

"I love you, too. When I get ready for work, I'll throw some things in a bag. When I get off in the morning, we can touch base. How does that sound?"

He nodded. "Good. I'll give you my house key. I've got a spare at home."

His phone vibrated.

"Don't get any big ideas about leaving me a 'to do' list, or anything." She chuckled at her own joke.

Tyson looked at his phone. It was a text from Deetz. He read it aloud to Callie: "We think Milligan paid us a visit too. Sounds like a real wingnut. I'll come by ASAP."

10

Sunny was awakened by the rumbling of the garage door chugging open.

Blaine.

He had his own garage door opener.

He always parked in the driveway, walked through the garage, and came in through the kitchen.

She laid perfectly still on the couch in the front room.

Her eyes were locked open. Her heart banged in her rib cage.

She forced herself to quickly get her bearings. She checked her watch: 4:40 p.m. She'd slept a long time. Everything for dinner was prepared; she'd made sure of that before she laid down to rest.

He was coming and she needed to make a quick decision: get up, greet him, and start serving him—or pretend to be asleep? If she did the latter, it would give him the opportunity to call her lazy and get him started on that tangent.

She sat up, hurried into the master bathroom, and turned on the water. She splashed her face, rinsed her mouth out, and patted her face dry with a towel.

Blaine clattered around loudly in the kitchen and she could barely breathe as she fixed her hair.

At least he didn't come straight for me.

She reapplied her plum lipstick with a trembling hand, then reached for her Daisy perfume.

"I told you, kiwi apple!" His yell and subsequent cussing from the kitchen carved a cavern in her chest.

It's starting.

She'd gotten him the peach nectarine Red Bull; it'd always been his favorite—

Oh my gosh . . . he told me he wanted a new flavor. Idiot!

She stared at herself in the mirror. Her face was almost completely healed from the last battering. She looked into her own brown eyes and wondered what she would look like the next time she glanced in that mirror.

Eying herself one last time, she breathed in as deeply as she could, exhaled, forced an exaggerated smile, and headed for the kitchen.

"HAVE I GOT A DINNER FOR YOU," Sunny said. "Marinated flank steak. Baked potatoes." She turned the corner to the kitchen and immediately noticed the rage in his eyes. "Tossed salad—"

"What the heck is *this*?" Blaine slammed the six-pack of Red Bull on the counter. "I told you, kiwi apple."

"I know, honey. I forgot." Sunny made herself chuckle. "You always get the peach nectarine. I'll return it tomorrow, no problem. How was your day?"

"What am I supposed to drink now?"

"How about if I make you some Gatorade? I have the powder mix."

"You don't listen to me." He stepped closer. "If you *listened*, if you *cared*, this would be kiwi apple." He picked up the six-pack and slammed it down again.

She had to get him off this. "Don't be ridiculous." Again, she laughed nervously as she crossed to the oven. "I care about you more than anything in the world, I just forgot, okay? I'm human. Now, let me get the potatoes going."

She was determined to stay busy, keep it upbeat, hold her own. She set the oven to four hundred and got the salad out of the fridge.

But she knew what was coming. There was no way he was *not* going to address the visit from Wayne Deetz.

"Would you take a look at this?" Sunny removed the foil

covering from the marinating flank steak and held it up to him. "Your very favorite."

Blaine looked at it with his small, frowning mouth, then tilted his head back with a scowl.

For an instant, it had pleased him, she could tell.

Keep it going. Keep it positive.

"I forget how long to broil this. Do you remember?" She leaned on the counter, picked up the recipe card, and pretended to read it again.

His silence had her trembling with fear.

She glanced over.

Oh no.

He was reaching up into what he called the "liquor cabinet," which he insisted she keep well stocked.

Not the gin . . .

"Crush me some ice," he said, clanking the bottle of Boodles on the counter and going to the cupboard for his favorite glass. "You got limes, I hope."

"Uh huh. Sure did." But each time he drank the fifty-proof gin he ended up enraged about something. She figured it was worth a try to change his mind. "I thought maybe a little red wine would be good with the red meat."

That was it.

He stopped, exaggeratedly.

"You thought? You *thought*. That was your *first* mistake."

"It's fine. Never mind. You know what you want—" She quickly crossed to the freezer and removed the tray of ice.

"*You thought* it was a good idea to spend the day with your *girl-friend*, Callie Freeland—"

"I didn't go. And she's not my girlfriend." Sunny feigned a laugh and got the ice to the sink. She hesitantly approached him to get his glass.

He ripped it away from her outstretched hands.

"*You thought* it was a good idea to have her cop friend come over—"

"Honey, that was something between Callie and him. She left her umbrella in his car or something like that. It had nothing to do with me."

He clacked the glass down and grabbed her wrists.

"No, Blaine." She tried to pull away, but it was impossible.

"You expect me to believe that? Huh?" Blaine shook her. "Why did he know my name? Huh?" With each 'huh,' he squeezed and twisted her wrists tighter.

"Stop Blaine. Stop. You're hurting me." She never knew what was coming—a backhand? A kick?

He gritted his teeth, wrenched her tighter, and pulled her close. He reeked of alcohol. She didn't even know where he'd been all day.

"What have you told Callie Freeland?"

"Nothing. I swear."

"Is she your lover?"

"That's crazy. Of course not. Stop it, Blaine. You're hurting me."

"I know she works at some shelter. God help me, Sunny, if you're planning on leaving, I'll find you. I'll kill you. You know I will."

He looked down at the floor, grimaced, and stomped on Sunny's left foot.

The pain was instant and raw. She screamed and tried to drop to the floor, grab the foot—but he still had her by the wrists.

"What. Have. You. Told. Her?" he enunciated each word like a psychopath.

Sunny was crying. "Let go. Let go, please. It hurts. I need to—"

"You answer me!"

She looked down. Her flimsy woven shoe was covered in blood. He'd crushed the top of her foot. She wondered if it was broken.

One of his hands released.

With it, he yanked the back of her hair, ripping her head upright.

She screamed as loudly as she could.

"Shut up!" He clamped the free hand over half her face. His satanic eyes were inches from hers. She couldn't breathe. His hand was massive and sweaty. Her left foot was swimming in blood.

In a flash, he twirled her around, locked her neck in the crook of his arm, covered her mouth, and dragged her into the bedroom.

"When I let go of your mouth, you are not going to scream," he said. "You scream again and you're dead. When I let go, you're going to calmly tell Blaine everything you've said to Callie Freeland about us. Do you understand?"

She could barely breathe. His massive arm cranked tighter against her throat. She was seeing stars and wheezing to get air. She could die, right there. *Tonight may be it. I should have listened to Callie.* She vowed then and there, if she escaped that night alive, she would be gone—move far, far away; maybe out of the country.

"Do you understand?" he yelled.

At his mercy, she shook her head up and down—not breathing anymore.

He shoved her as he let go of her mouth.

She gasped and gulped and choked for air.

He bashed the back of her head. "Stop it!"

She was only trying to stay alive now. "Let go of my neck," she managed.

He released his big arm from choking.

She wheezed for air.

Dizzy.

Stars.

She realized she was flickering in and out of consciousness.

He flipped her over on the bed like a doll, stomach down, and whipped her right arm around behind her back, and shoved it as high as it would go toward her neck.

"Ahhh!" she screamed.

"Talk!"

Her face was buried in the sheets amid a smear of tears and snot.

He grabbed her hair and whipped her head back.

"If you don't tell me what you told Callie Freeland, you're going to die. Tonight. Right here. Are you ready to die?"

He pulled her head back so far that she could see a portion of the ceiling fan.

"Nothing," she blurted. "I've said nothing."

"Then what's a cop doing here?" He drilled a knee into her back, hitting a nerve.

The pain shot down her legs like a lightning bolt.

She retched.

"Don't you *dare* throw up," he commanded.

"Stop, stop . . . I'll talk. Stop hurting me. Please, please, I beg you."

He released her.

He was on his feet.

He grabbed her by the back of her shirt and forced her to her feet. Both shoes had come off and her left foot was a bloody mess.

He dragged her into the front room. Her shirt ripped. She couldn't put weight on the bad foot. He shoved her onto the couch.

"Stay right there."

He huffed off to the kitchen.

Run! Out the front door.

No use. He'd catch me in four steps.

He was back. With the bottle of gin. He groaned as he sat down on the coffee table in front of the couch. He swigged the gin and said, "Talk."

"She's noticed the bruising," Sunny said, crying. "Her boyfriend used to . . . hit her. She knows the signs. She's talked about the shelter where she volunteers."

Blaine suddenly shifted over to the couch, making Sunny flinch.

He held the bottle in his left hand, leaned over her, and ran the back of his hand along her cheek.

"I've told her nothing about you . . . us, how—"

"Why was the cop here, then?" He ran his hand up to her hair and yanked.

Sunny squirmed. "Maybe because she suspects something. I didn't ask for him to come. It won't happen again. I promise."

He tugged her hair again, hard. Then he made a fist and gently banged it against her chin, her forehead, her cheeks.

"You're going to end your little fling with Callie, aren't you?" His little fake punches got harder.

She was nodding before he finished speaking.

"And if there's any more contact from Deetz . . . ." The little punches began to hurt. "You're going to tell him to leave you alone, that you're in a happy relationship, aren't you?"

Sunny nodded profusely, only trying to stay alive.

And if she did live, she would do so for one purpose—to regain her freedom.

"Good." He slapped her face.

It stung hot.

"Now, get in there and make this dinner you're bragging about."

11

———————

By the time Deetz arrived at Callie's condo it was getting dark. Callie had left to work her nightshift at the grocery warehouse and Tyson had met him at his car, walked him in, and showed him where Blaine Milligan allegedly doused the hallway and door with gasoline. Deetz took pictures on his phone.

Together, the men examined the red gas can Milligan left behind, then stood on Callie's balcony overlooking the shimmering Willamette River.

Deetz took in the cool night air and city lights below. He was flat out exhausted, hungry, and just wanted to be home with Joanie. The police protestors at headquarters were growing in number and becoming more violent; he was afraid he might get called back in.

"Do you want to talk with the neighbor lady who saw him?" Tyson said.

Deetz looked at his watch. "Not now. You told me everything she saw, right?"

"I think so, yeah. And she confirmed it was him when we showed her his photo."

"Right. I've got her name. I can call her if I need to. I've got photos of everything. I'll put it all in my report in the morning. I'm most interested in the security camera footage," Deetz said.

"I'll have Callie get you a number to call ASAP."

Deetz nodded.

"She's really concerned about Sunny," Tyson said. "She texted me from work and said Sunny's not responding to her texts; she tried to call her—no answer."

Deetz shook his head, thinking about Blaine Milligan's long rap sheet. He'd intended to stop at Sunny's on his way home to make sure she was okay, and to put Milligan on warning, if he was there —but the day had gotten away from him.

"You staying here tonight?" Deetz said.

"I'm going home. Callie works till morning. She packed a bag. I think she should stay at my place. What do you think?"

Deetz nodded while tapping away at his phone. "I'm not an alarmist, but this guy's a bad seed." He filled Tyson in on Blaine Milligan's criminal history. He also told him about the trash bags missing from his house.

"That settles that," Tyson said. "Callie can stay with me as long as she needs to."

"Can you hang around till my print guy gets here?" Deetz said, looking at his phone. "Be about twenty minutes."

"Absolutely," Tyson said. "Thanks for arranging it."

Perhaps it was the sirens below, but something got them talking about the protesters.

"They're setting up tents now near Pioneer Square. They want an autonomous zone," Deetz said.

"Freedom to govern themselves, huh?" Tyson said. "We'll see how that works for them."

"It's a different world than it was even just ten years ago. I don't have any grandkids yet, but I feel sorry for 'em. The America I grew up with is disappearing fast."

"It's got to be tough, being a cop right now," Tyson said. "What's the mindset of your team? Is morale really low?"

"I've never seen it like this in thirty-four years," Deetz said. "It's totally depressing. But it's been a long-time coming. There are some bad cops here and there, have been forever. Now, the masses are speaking out. They want change, and that has to come from the top. I'm open to it, if it makes us better. There's always room for improvement."

Deetz walked back into the condo and Tyson followed.

"We've got kids from my school who've been arrested," Tyson

said.

"It's a free-for-all. We don't have enough people to staff it," Deetz said. "Luckily, during the day it calms down some, but at night, man, it's volatile. There's a lot of hatred flying in all directions."

"Our pastor talked about it Sunday," Tyson said. "He mentioned those verses that say, 'because of the increase of wickedness, the love of most will grow cold.' That really hit me, because when I see all the violence, looting, and burning, my natural reaction is anger."

"Preaching to the choir," Deetz said. "We gotta be better than that. I'm guilty."

They made a bit more small-talk and Deetz showed himself out.

As he maneuvered his way through the parking deck in the Subaru, he called Joanie on speakerphone. She was watching the protests on the news. She started to tell him the dentist recommended having Leena's wisdom teeth removed.

"Okay, we'll talk about it, but right now I need to tell you something." Deetz knew she was going to be upset. He took a deep breath and quickly brought her up to speed on the gas incident at Callie's condo, and on Blaine Milligan's rap sheet.

Joanie was shocked. She began to chime in about how "creepy" Milligan looked on his Facebook page.

"Honey," Deetz interrupted, "I'm telling you all this because I need to stop at Sunny's house."

"Not now?" Joanie squawked.

"I'm going to make sure she's okay and—"

"What if he's there? Wayne, do this in the daytime."

"If he's there, I'm putting him on warning—about the gas at Callie's, taking our trash, and abusing Sunny."

"Why don't you do this in the morning? Come home. Get a good night's sleep. Stop on your way in tomorrow."

"Callie's concerned about Sunny after Milligan saw me there this morning. She's tried to reach her all day and heard nothing. I can't ignore this; I wouldn't sleep a wink. It's not like I'm Joe Public going in there. This is a police matter."

"I swear, you're a workaholic. You love this stuff."

"No, I don't. I'm starved. I'm tired. I want to come home. This is business. This girl may be in trouble. It's my job to serve and protect. I need to at least check in on her."

There was a long silence.

"Hello?" Deetz said, trying to calm her down.

"You better go up there with badge out and gun drawn."

12

———

Deetz eased the Subaru to a stop in front of Sunny's house. It was dark and cool, approaching 8 p.m. Milligan's obnoxious truck was nowhere in sight; that was a relief. But it didn't necessarily mean he wasn't inside. The garage door was closed, and several lamps cast a yellow glow inside the small house. One would assume it was a quiet, happy abode.

Deetz guessed otherwise.

He withdrew the Glock from his leather chest holster, racked the slide, and holstered it. He then got out, locked the car, and headed up the driveway, withdrawing his leather badge case as he walked. A beautiful fall night.

At the front door, he rang the doorbell once, rehearsed what he would say, and reminded himself to get a good look around once inside.

After about forty-five seconds of seeing and hearing no movement inside, he rang the doorbell again.

This time, he noticed the wisp of a shadow move across the floor down the hallway.

He knocked hard. "Sunny, it's Wayne Deetz, Portland PD," he yelled. "I just want to talk for a second."

Nothing.

He knocked again, harder. "I know you're in there, Sunny. Please open up for one minute."

A dark figure appeared at the end of the hall. It stopped and stood still. Deetz was almost sure it was her.

"Just give me one minute," Deetz yelled, up close to the door.

The figure shrugged and came toward him.

The door opened three inches.

"What?" Sunny's eyes were bloodshot. Her forehead, sweaty. She was agitated. She eyed his gun.

Deetz held the badge up to her. "Can I come in? This is an official police matter."

Her eyes darted up and down the street, similar to the way they had that morning. *She's worried Milligan will show up.*

"I'll only stay a minute," he said.

She unlocked a chain latch and the door opened.

He holstered his weapon and stepped inside. "Oh boy, something smells good," he said.

"What can I do for you? Make it quick." Sunny held the door open with both hands and stood with all her weight on her right foot. Slippers covered both feet. She wore jeans and a black long-sleeve shirt with the sleeves pushed up to her elbows.

Deetz could sense, without a doubt, something had happened there—recently. He needed to look around. Without asking, he stepped into the front room.

"Hold up." Sunny limped into the front room, which was lit by a lamp on an end table.

"What happened?" He eyed her foot as she leaned against the wall.

"What do you want, officer? I'm in a hurry."

"Are you going somewhere?" Deetz noticed dark spots on the carpet.

Sunny saw him looking at the floor.

"I've got a show on." She feigned a laugh. "Just winding down for the day."

"What happened to your foot?" Deetz said, evenly.

"Nothing. Just stubbed a toe, right before you got here. Still smarting."

"Your wrists are raw," Deetz said. "And I'm assuming that's blood on the carpet." He walked into the kitchen.

"Wait! You can't just go anywhere you want."

"If I suspect a crime, I can." He saw a bottle of gin on the counter, with about a third left in it. Dirty dishes filled the area all around the sink. He looked into the adjacent room and saw an unkempt bed and more dark spots on the carpet. An overnight bag lay open on the bed.

"Tell me what happened here, Sunny."

She hobbled in and leaned against the doorframe. She favored her right arm. From the light of the kitchen, he could see that her throat was blotchy.

Deetz fumed.

She's been beaten to a pulp.

"If you're done, I really need to get to bed. Work tomorrow."

"You can tell me, Sunny. You can trust me. I'll help to protect you. I know he did this."

She shook her head in denial. "I've had a rough day, that's all. Please go now."

"There's no excuse for this, Sunny. No matter what he says or how he tries to spin it, this is abuse. He'll go to prison."

"Sir," she held up a hand to stop him. "This is my house. It's none of your business what goes on here. I'm handling it, okay. I've made a decision. I'm handling it. Now, please, leave. Please, before he comes back. You have to trust me on this."

Deetz walked toward the bedroom.

"Stop!" she yelled.

There was blood on the comforter and what he assumed was a small clump of Sunny's hair on the bed.

He turned around.

She had not followed him.

"This is a crime scene, Sunny. I want you to file a report, right now, with me. I'll walk you through it. We can get you to a safe house tonight."

"You see that bag in there. I'm leaving. *Tonight.*"

"This is your house!" Deetz said. "Don't let him drive you into the night, on the run. Send him to jail."

"For how long? How long is he gonna get? Huh? You tell the truth. Two months? One month? One dang week?"

She works for the government. She knows what she's talking about. I could arrest Milligan and he could be out on bail within hours. Even if they did hold him and convict him, she was right, it wouldn't be for long. Unless he was raping her. That would make a difference.

"Sunny just be honest with me and I'll be honest with you. What happened here? He was mad I was here this morning and he took it out on you? Beat you up? Is that right?"

She glared at him with eyes on fire and nostrils flaring. "I don't trust anyone right now. I just want you to leave. Will you just *go* so I can pack and get out of here? That's how you can help me."

"You know what he did today? He doused Callie's door and hallway with gas and left a gas can threatening to burn her down. He took trash bags from the garbage can at my house."

Sunny's head dropped and her shoulders shook. She limped to the counter and leaned over, crying. Deetz could see a small bald spot and blood on the top of her head.

"Sunny, has he raped you?"

She immediately glared at him. "We're done!"

"He beats you, obviously."

She nodded and cried. "He's bipolar."

"Let me arrest him, Sunny," Deetz pleaded. "If you don't think he'll do enough time then at least it will give you time to formulate a plan."

Leaning on the counter with both elbows she ran her hands through her hair, shook her head, and cursed.

"I can take a formal report right now," Deetz said. "And if we can nail him on stalking or threatening Callie, that will add to his time. There are security cameras. Plus, he has a rap sheet a mile long, so this will—"

"Stop!" Sunny looked up, her face smeared with tears. "I'm sorry, sir . . . officer Deetz. Thank you for trying to help me, really. But you need to go, now. No one understands Blaine Milligan like I do. He will not stop—"

"Sunny, please—"

"No! Enough! I'm not filing a report. Now, please, leave. That's how you can help me. If he pulls in right now, we're *both* dead."

She turned and hopped on one foot toward the front door.

Deetz followed, noticing fresh blood droplets on the wood floor.

Her left foot was dripping blood.
She could barely lift her right arm.
Deetz raged inside.
He had to find Blaine Milligan—before he did any more harm.

13

STANDING at her locker adjacent to the break room in the grocery warehouse, Callie threw a thick, gray hoodie on over the Ducks' sweatshirt she was already wearing. Her mind was on a million things as she adjusted her wide, purple headband in the mirror, which covered her ears on cool nights like this one.

On her way out to the loading dock she got her leather work gloves out of her back pocket and started putting them on. When she worked she always left her engagement ring from Cooper home in a dish on her dresser. She was thinking about all she still had to do for the wedding—nail down a spring date and venue, find a dress, book a band, figure out the guest list, food, photography. Combine all that with the fact she had this maniac Blaine Milligan threatening to burn her place to the ground and she suddenly felt a bit overwhelmed.

She heard her name being called.

It was her manager, Edgar, waving her down.

"You headed for the dock?" he said.

"Yes, sir."

"Good. Alford's running late. Sorry. He's on his way; ETA is like twenty minutes."

"No problem."

"How's Cooper?" Edgar said.

She smiled. "Good. Thanks."

"Glad to be back teaching?"

"Oh, yeah. It's where he belongs. How's your family?"

"Okay, except my daughter's a cop and it ain't safe to be a cop in this town right now."

"Oh, that's right. Jillian, isn't it? I met her at the company picnic."

"Yeah, Jillian. We still call her Jilly. She's been on the force four years. Used to love going to work. Loved what she did. Now, she's thinking about going back to school. It's a shame. If this keeps up we won't have any cops left."

Callie kept thinking about the gasoline doused outside her door. She thought she could still smell it; or was that her mind just playing tricks?

"I hope she stays safe and things get better soon." Her mind was so scrambled, that was about all she could think to say.

They started to part ways and Edgar said, "Where's your helmet?"

"I left it at the dock."

"You wear that helmet now. Tell Alford to wear his—he's always trying to buck the system."

"Will do."

She felt the cool wind as she approached the open loading dock area. She couldn't shake the memory of the red gas can and its eerie message: *Next time I light it.*

All she could do was trust God. Leave it in his hands.

She popped a peppermint, took her left glove off, and dug her phone out of the hip pocket of her snug jeans.

A loud honk surprised her from behind. It was her friend, Moncrief, whizzing by on one of the forklifts. They waved.

She looked back at her phone and a text from Cooper awaited her: "Deetz took photos of everything. I need a number to call at your condo to get access to security cam footage. Yep there are cameras! He'll file a report in the morning. He said you need to stay at my place. Police orders ha ha ha."

She chuckled.

She loved him so much.

There was still nothing from Sunny. That worried her. But she dare not reach out to her again knowing Blaine's evil eyes were everywhere.

She examined the semitruck that was backed up to the dock. She guessed there were still about forty boxes that needed to be unloaded. She liked the physical work, especially on cool nights like this. And she considered it as good as a workout.

She forwarded the contact information for her condo management to Tyson with a quick text that read, "Love ya." Then she got her other glove back on, fetched her helmet, and walked out to the edge of the dock and put it on. She tightened the strap, took in a deep breath to psych herself up for the work ahead, and . . .

Headlights flashed on and off in the distance.

Her heart stopped.

She pretended not to see it and continued fiddling with her helmet strap.

The lights flashed again, twice this time—*on off, on off.*

It looked like a large pickup truck and it was parked all alone in the loading and unloading zone.

She backed up slowly, rounded the corner, and stepped onto the bed of the semi, out of sight of the vehicle.

Her heart pounded like pistons. Deetz had said Blaine Milligan was in a pickup truck when they met that morning, but he didn't say what color.

She bent over, breathing in and out deeply.

Keep cool. It's probably someone you know. It has to be a co-worker. Blaine Milligan couldn't get in here. It's employees only.

Callie steadied herself, crossed to the side of the semi, and slowly tilted her head so one eye could see the vehicle. White pickup. Windows down. Smoke wafting up into the night from the driver's window. She couldn't see the driver.

She moved back into the bed of the truck, ripped a glove off, and called Tyson.

He answered with some smart aleck comment about her staying at his place, police orders.

"What color's Milligan's truck?" was all she said.

Tyson got serious instantly. "White. Why? What's going on? You're at work, right?"

"Yeah. I'm on the dock." She found herself out of breath and her voice was trembling. "There's a white truck parked way out in the back. It's flashing its lights at me."

"Wait, he couldn't get back there, though—right?"

"Unless he went off-road and drove around the gate."

"Who's with you?"

She could hear Tyson was in motion.

"Nobody's directly with me right now. But I'm fine in here, I guess. Edgar's here. Moncrief. Another guy's supposed to help me in a minute."

She walked back over to the side of the semi and slowly peered around the corner.

The truck was gone.

"You stay right there. I'm coming," Tyson said.

"Hold on, Cooper. It's gone. He's gone. Thank God. Hold on." She breathed a sigh of relief and crept to the other side of the truck, still thinking she smelled gas, or something. She slowly peered around the back corner so she could see the other side of the lot.

Her insides detonated.

Blaine Milligan, who she recognized from social media, stood in the back of his truck, which was backed in just thirty yards away.

"Dear Jesus." She scooped her head back into the truck and froze, unable to breathe.

"What?" Tyson called into the phone. "Is he gone?"

Callie couldn't move. She was trying to figure out if what she saw was even real.

"Callie. Talk to me!" Tyson yelled from the phone.

She slowly lifted the phone to her ear. "It's him! He moved the truck closer," she whispered. "He's standing in back holding an assault rifle. There're more guns at his feet." And he had a cigar stuffed in the corner of his mouth.

"Callie, shut the bay door and go tell Edgar, right now! Stay with him," Tyson yelled. "Have him lock it all down. I'm calling 911 and Deetz. I'm on my way, okay? I'm coming!"

"Okay." She jammed the phone in her pocket, jumped off the back of the semi, and ran for the big, bright red button that opened and closed the huge metal door. Without hesitation, she smashed the button and held it down.

The loud motor for the door rumbled to life, the chains began clanking and twisting, and the door started down.

Callie realized she was still holding the button. She took her hand off and stood there willing the door to go down faster, faster.

When it was almost closed, she heard him yell something and the night air beyond the door exploded with bone-jarring gunfire.

Callie dropped to the concrete floor, curled into a ball, covered her head and ears with both arms, and waited breathlessly for the gunfire to stop.

14

FROM THE WINDOW in her front room, Sunny watched Wayne Deetz drive away. When his car's taillights were out of sight, she limped as fast as she could down the hall, through the kitchen, and into the bedroom. She turned around and dropped onto the bed, wincing in pain.

Everything hurt—her back, foot, arm, wrists, scalp. Her left slipper was soaked in blood and dripping profusely. She removed it gingerly, revealing a gooey, bruised mess atop her foot. It hurt so badly and it needed to be cleaned and properly bandaged, but first she needed to get the heck out of there before Blaine showed up.

She leaned back on the bed, grabbed a pillow, and ripped the pillowcase off. Groaning in pain, she gathered a clump of bedsheet and applied pressure to the foot wound. She wrapped it as tightly as she could with the pillowcase and secured it by tying a knot, screaming out in pain as she did.

Next, she rolled over—her right arm on fire with pain—got her phone out of her pocket and found the photo Callie had texted showing the getaway list.

If he'd have found this, I'd be dead.

She studied the list, then noticed something dark to her right.

No.

That can't be . . .

She reached over and picked it up.

It was her hair.

Involuntarily, she retched. She scrambled to the side of the bed and heaved again, violently, but nothing came up; she'd eaten virtually nothing of the famous dinner. Her whole body throbbed in pain.

She reached up, gently touched where her scalp burned, and looked at her fingers—wet with blood. She grabbed more bedsheet, gently dotted the wound, and tossed the sheet aside.

I should be in the ER.

Wherever she was going, she'd need to find a doctor.

Sunny grimaced as she got to her feet and limped into the master closet. She wanted to check the front of the house to see if there was any sign of Blaine, but it would hurt too much and take too long. She dropped to the floor of the closet and grunted as she shoved a large stack of sheets and towels off the big plastic container she referred to as her "everything box."

She had trouble getting the lid off. As she gritted her teeth and struggled with it, she noticed her torn wrists. It made her so angry she practically tore the top off the tub. She pitched the lid aside with fury and began rifling through the contents.

Working quickly and frantically she set aside everything important she could find—paperwork for the house, birth certificate, social security card, and a folder in which she kept all of her banking information. Leaving the container open, she crawled back to the bed and stuffed the paperwork into the overnight bag.

What will happen to the house?

She knew the only way she would ever be able to return would be if Blaine was in prison—or dead.

Leaning on the bed, she got to her feet, hopped to her dresser, and threw various clothes over to the bag. Next, she limped into the closet, grabbed various pants and tops, and got them to the bag.

Sweating and out of breath, she made it to the bathroom, got her cosmetic bag with trembling hands, and threw in necessities; everything else she could get later, wherever she ended up.

She constantly listened for Blaine.

If he shows up now, this will literally be my last day on earth.

Callie had once asked her what she thought about the afterlife— heaven, hell, all that. She'd told her she didn't believe in any of it;

she believed you just went to sleep. She wasn't ready to find out today if she was right or wrong.

For now, she would drive east. That's all she knew. She could figure out where, specifically, later.

What will they think at work?

Rumors would swirl.

Once she got based somewhere, she would call them, apologize, tell them the truth about her situation and what had happened.

She would also call Deetz and tell him everything about Blaine Milligan. Sunny had thought of this moment a million times but had never had the guts to go.

Well now you're doing it. No turning back.

Her phone buzzed from the bed.

Him!

Her heart lurched.

She hobbled from the bathroom to the bed and patted and scrambled furiously until she found the glowing phone beneath the covers and read the message—from Blaine: "Having fun with your pal Callie."

"No!" Sunny screamed and pounded the bed.

Her immediate impulse was to call Callie, but there was no time.

She had to go.

Let her be okay.

She'd call her once on the road.

The phone vibrated again. Another text from Blaine: "Let's watch a movie. Find something you like. Be there soon."

She stopped in her tracks—thinking, thinking, thinking.

She could unpack really quickly. He'd never know she'd planned to leave. Watch a movie. Make up. *It would be okay.*

Just like always, he would calm down—for a while.

She examined her surroundings—the room in shambles. The clump of her hair on the bed. Blood everywhere.

Your blood.

From head to toe she felt broken. Hurt. Weak.

Give this up. Do what he says. You can't get away from him. He'll find you. You know he'll find you.

Her phone rang.

It was Callie.

Sunny answered quickly. "Are you okay?"

Callie spoke firmly and directly. "You need to get out of there *right now*, Sunny. Get your keys and drive! He's a maniac."

"What did he do to you?"

"Came to my work. Fired a gun in the air. Go Sunny. Go to the Dorcas House. You know where it is. Go now!"

"I'm going east."

"Go. Now! He left here like ten minutes ago. Get out *now*."

That settled it.

Callie had always been the voice of reason.

"I will. Sorry, Callie. Sorry about everything."

"Go, Sunny. I'll see you on the other side, girl."

Sunny shoved the phone in her back pocket, checked the contents of the overnight bag one last time, and zipped it closed. She hit the floor, crawled to the closet, and found her favorite casual shoes. She put the right one on, took the left one back to the bag and slipped it inside.

Grunting, she got to her feet, grabbed the bag, and hobbled out to the kitchen. She got her purse and keys and took one last look around.

"Bye, house," she whispered.

In the closet near the door to the garage she grabbed a coat. She opened the door and dragged everything into the garage, sweating, limping as fast as she could to the Ford Focus. She opened the passenger door, tossed the overnight bag on the floor, the coat and purse onto the seat.

Her heart hammered as she slammed the door, leaned on the car, and limped quickly around to the driver's side. As she opened the door and got in she cursed, realizing she would have to push the clutch pedal with her injured foot.

There's no way!

Again, she considered hurrying back inside and unpacking before Blaine got there.

She sat there in the driver's seat, head down, thinking, on the verge of going back in.

Callie's words came back: "You need to get out of there right now, Sunny. Get your keys and drive! He's a maniac."

There, someone else knew.

Someone on the outside could see, finally, could confirm what she was up against.

"Maniac."

She slammed the door, jammed the keys in the ignition, and started the car. She hit the clutch pedal with her right foot, put it in reverse, and quickly used the same foot to hit the gas. The Focus stalled out.

She tried again with one foot and stalled out.

Heck with this.

She started the car again, braced for pain, and eased her left foot down on the clutch. It felt like bones were breaking in her foot, but she got it in reverse.

No turning back now.

She backed down the slope, stopped, and looked both ways at the end of the driveway.

Clear.

She was about to back into the street when it hit her—she'd not turned off the Find My Friends app on her phone. Blaine had always forced her to keep it on, so he knew where she was at all times. She ripped her phone out, found Find My Friends and turned it off. Shaking uncontrollably, she flicked into Settings and turned off Location Services and every other switch she could find that had anything to do with finding Sunny Carlisle.

She let out a sigh of relief and looked both ways again. A car was coming way in the distance, but she had time to get out.

Using her injured left foot for the clutch, she grimaced and scooted backward, bouncing the Focus into the street. The car coming up behind her was coming faster than she'd gauged. Again, she cried out in pain as she hit the clutch and shifted into first and got going.

The car behind her bore right down on her tail, flashed its lights and honked. For a petrifying moment she thought it was Blaine, but it was a sedan, not his high-riding truck. Besides, he'd be coming from the opposite direction if he'd been at Callie's warehouse.

With gut-wrenching pain in her left foot, she finally got the car into second, then third, and got it moving along. The guy behind her backed off slightly so she could breathe.

It was starting to rain and she was cold. She turned on her wipers and the heat, and retraced her steps leaving the house. She went through everything she'd brought with her, hoping she'd covered all her bases.

Blaine will go ballistic.

Her phone settings were off so there was no way he could find her.

You're free.

Her tentative plan was to fill up with gas and head out of Portland eastbound on I-84. Eventually, she would need to choose between staying on that toward Idaho or taking I-82 north toward Spokane; but she was leaning toward Idaho and east from there, simply because she was sick of the Pacific Northwest and the bad memories she'd made there.

She'd grown up in Twisp, Washington, where her father was a ranger for the National Park Service and her mother was a seamstress. Her older brother Bobby was a chemical salesman in Fort Worth and her twin sister, Isabelle, was a commercial flight attendant based in L.A.

She usually got gas at the Chevron up ahead, but Blaine knew that and she wasn't going to take the chance of him spotting her. She would stop at the Shell just a few miles before the highway.

It was dark and drizzling. She'd been watching for Blaine's truck in the lane of oncoming cars. With each pickup she passed she held her breath.

So far, so good.

She tapped her thumbs on the wheel and smiled, almost tasting freedom—but she knew well she was not out of the woods yet. She would feel better after fueling up and getting on the interstate.

Would he guess she was heading east and come after her?

His street-smarts worried her. Somehow, he was always just there.

She wished she had a weapon, a gun, a knife, something. Because, if he did manage to find her, she would be in the fight of her life.

That can't happen.

Another pickup came toward her, a big one. Light colored.

Please, no.

She willed herself to disappear in the driver's seat, for him not to recognize her—but he knew her car . . .

The vehicle approaching looked just like his mammoth truck.

She lifted a hand to her head to hide herself.

In a rainy flash, she saw his face.

He was scowling and jabbing a finger at her.

The image was seared in her mind as she kept driving.

His mouth had been moving, as if he was talking to her as their eyes locked and they passed each other in the mist.

Sunny's whole body shuddered.

"No, no, no, no!" She eyed the rearview mirror, adjusted it, told herself to breathe.

His huge red brake lights lit up the rainy night.

His truck lurched off road.

He's coming.

15

———

Deetz hadn't been home long and was eating leftover roasted chicken at the kitchen table with Joanie. It was getting late and he needed sleep.

She got up from the table. "How about some fruit or bread with that?" As was her way, she went ahead and microwaved a piece of garlic toast before he'd answered.

Wearing her pink flannel pajamas, she set the bread on his plate, sat down, filled him in a bit more on Leena's dentist visit, then told him the latest on son J.P. and girlfriend Tammy.

"They were downtown last night," she hesitated, "at the protest."

Deetz set his fork down, told himself to keep his cool, and stared at her. "What?"

"You heard me, Wayne." She tilted her head.

"What were they protesting?" He was infuriated.

"Wayne don't be that way. You know what."

"Police brutality? Are you kidding me? Defunding the police— where his dad works? What the heck?"

"You know Tammy has a heart for—"

"For what? For who? Those anarchists burning down our city?"

Joanie stood. "I'm not going to talk to you until you calm down."

She went to the sink.

"Portland PD *paid* for his education. They've given me a livelihood for thirty-four years. How dare he."

"This isn't about you, Wayne," Joanie said, putting away clean dishes from the dish rack. "Everything's not about you."

"I can't tell you three people in our department who are prejudiced."

"This is a national thing. It's a movement. Their generation wants change."

"Yeah, and it's stripping our country of its history and heritage."

"Like I said, I won't talk to you when you're in this state."

"You know how dangerous it is down there? Is he back down there tonight? I'm calling him." Deetz said.

"Don't call him, Wayne. He's twenty-four—"

"He's acting like he's twelve."

She shook her head in disgust. "You're the one acting like a twelve-year-old. My gosh, grow up. They're adults. They can do what they want."

"I suppose they want autonomous zones."

"They want police to stop racial profiling and abusing and killing innocent Black people. And they're speaking out about it, peacefully. You know that."

He'd completely lost his appetite.

"They're trying to burn down the Federal Courthouse. That's okay with you?"

"J.P. and Tammy aren't part of that."

"Six of our guys are in the hospital; one might lose his sight from lasers being burned into his eyes. They're pelting us with garbage and bottles. They're throwing Molotov cocktails and firing mortars at us. They're lighting fires everywhere. This is just an excuse for lawlessness."

"I'm not going to listen to this. You're mad at the wrong people." She went about putting dishes and glasses away, loudly.

"Who do those people think they're going to win over by spray painting statues and public property, and destroying the city?"

"That's not what J.P.'s doing. It's two totally different things. You're just mad, that's all. Don't take it out on J.P. and Tammy."

"It's the attitude, okay? How dare they assume I'm prejudiced? How dare they lump everyone into the same category? Who are they to judge? They've got their own problems. Do you know what those *peaceful* protestors are doing? They're going around to every business owner and demanding they put up racial diversity signs in their windows—or else they'll burn them down. How's that for peaceful?"

"Listen to yourself, Wayne. You sound like a bitter old man. My gosh. Cool down."

"I love this city and they're destroying it. And they're hurting innocent officers. It's ugly. It's downright evil. There were fifteen murders in Portland last month. Fifteen!"

"You better not have this attitude with J.P. or we're going to have a family feud on our hands. You need to just calm down and get some sleep."

He was worked up, for sure. She was right about that. The whole thing—the rioting, looting, destruction, and harm to his co-workers—had taken a toll on him. He needed to put this day in the books.

Joanie finished in the kitchen and said, "I'll see you in there," and went into the master bedroom. "Put the garage door down," she called and closed the doors.

Deetz rinsed his plate and silverware, put them in the dish-washer, and walked out onto the dark back porch, which he did often before bed, just to get some fresh air and reflect on the day.

It was cold and windy. He could feel drizzle blowing in from outside. He had so much on his mind—the explosive situation downtown, J.P.'s involvement, Sunny Carlisle's safety, the threat to Callie, and Blaine Milligan.

Deetz got a chill recalling how confrontational Milligan had been that morning in front of Sunny's house. And to text Callie? And send her a Friend Request? Pour gas and leave a threat, knowing it was obvious who did it? The guy was a runaway train.

Deetz contemplated calling J.P. and thought about what he would say; but in his current frame of mind, Joanie was right, it would inevitably lead to an argument. And there was far too much to be said in a text message. Often the boys would get into discussions with him via text and he would end up getting frustrated and calling them, thinking it was ridiculous to be typing out what should be a conversation. He decided to wait to contact J.P.

He went inside and turned out the kitchen lights, closed the garage door, and went into the study to turn out his desk lamp. His computer was still on and it dawned on him that he should double check their credit card accounts again, since the trash had gone missing.

He sat down and went to the bookmark for their secondary credit card company, logged in, and found no unusual activity. He then went to the website for the credit card they used most, which earned cash back, and the amount due immediately looked off—way too high. His face went flush. He scrolled down to recent activity and, with his heart ticking faster, he discovered a transaction that day at Black Iron Armory for $2277.56.

Guns.

He bought guns—or weapons of some kind—with our credit card.

"Low life scum." Deetz went over, quietly shut the door to the study, found the phone number, and called the credit card company. He knew his blood pressure must be through the roof. After working his way through a bunch of frustrating recordings and prompts, he got a live person and explained what had happened. Of course, she transferred him to another department.

Deetz's left ear buzzed with anxiety.

Help me get this straightened out. I need sleep so badly.

He could barely understand the next gentleman he got, who sounded like he was transmitting from the moon. He was able to explain what happened and the man opened a case for him and said they would be investigating. If all went as expected, Deetz would be credited for the purchase in question, hopefully within ten to fourteen days.

There was a soft knock at the study door and Joanie opened and came in. "Who are you talking to?"

He explained what had happened.

"There's nothing more you can do now." She turned and left. "Come to bed."

His phone buzzed.

It was a text from Tyson Cooper: "You still up?"

What now!

Deetz questioned whether the day would ever end. He wanted to ignore the text, but he couldn't.

"Yes," he texted back.

Seconds later his phone rang. Tyson anxiously explained he was with Callie at the warehouse where she worked. Blaine Milligan had driven his truck around the security gate, parked at the rear of the building where the loading docks were, and had his eye on Callie; flicked his lights at her. He then fired an assault rifle into the air and took off the same way he'd come in.

Tyson was furious.

Deetz urged him to calm down and inquired about security cameras. Tyson said the security team at the warehouse fully expected they would have it all on video and they were working on it.

"What can we do about this guy, Wayne? He can easily find out where I live. And we're concerned about Sunny. She's not answering her phone. You've got to get this guy."

"She was packing to get out of there when I saw her." Deetz filled Tyson in on his visit to Sunny's earlier. "Hopefully she got out on time."

"Where was she going?"

"She wouldn't say."

"I'm tempted to go to her house and see if he's there," Tyson said. "We're not going to be able to rest until—"

"Don't do that, Tyson. Nothing good's going to come out of that," Deetz said. "Is Callie going home with you now?"

"Yeah, they're letting her go for the night."

"Keep your weapon at your side and sleep with one eye open. I'm going to do the same. Between the video of him dousing Callie's place, the gas can, and tonight's video from the warehouse, we'll have plenty to arrest him on. Then I'm hoping Sunny will press charges." He explained more about the bloody fight scene at Sunny's home earlier that evening.

"For now, I need to get some sleep," Deetz said. "I'll be on it first thing in the morning, okay? Trust me."

He stood to end the call and heard a commotion break out on Tyson's end of the line. He thought he heard Callie's panicked voice in the background.

Tyson came back on. "Wayne, Milligan spotted Sunny on the

road as she was leaving town. He's after her—right now! She just called Callie, freaking out."

Deetz dropped his head in exhaustion. "Where?" he said.

Tyson said to Callie, "Where is she?"

"Mount Tabor," Callie said.

"I heard," Deetz said. "Text me Sunny's number. I'm on my way."

16

Sunny's hands clamped the steering wheel like a vice. The instant she'd seen Blaine go off road to turn around, she took the next right and called Callie. Since then, she'd frantically taken several more turns to lose Blaine, but she knew him . . . somehow, he would find her. He always did.

She could barely breathe.

If he finds me now, bag packed, leaving him—I die.

She swallowed the bile at the base of her throat and concentrated on keeping the car in her lane amidst the steady rain. She drove as fast as she safely could and was somewhat comforted by the number of cars on the road.

Find My Friends was turned off, so how could he possibly find her?

Her plans to get gas and jump on I-84 were out the window, because there's no way she was about to stop like a sitting duck to fill up her tank at a fully lit gas station. And because of the turns she'd made she was heading in the opposite direction of the interstate.

She thought of the shelter. Callie had given her the address—it was in her phone.

Sunny felt for her phone and, looking back and forth from her phone to the wet road, scrolled through her contacts.

Her phone rang in her hand and scared her—she almost dropped it. A wave of terror paralyzed her.

It's Blaine.

But a glance at the caller ID said it was Wayne Deetz. She quickly answered on speaker.

"Callie told me he's after you." Deetz got right to the point. "Is that still the case?"

"Yes, thank you . . . thank you for calling." Her own trembling voice surprised her, how scared she sounded. She cleared her throat and tried to be strong. "I'm on Klondike Drive. He saw me and turned around. He's coming."

Her resolve weakened and she cried silently.

"Do you see him behind you?" Deetz said.

Sunny looked in the rearview mirror, sniffed, took a deep breath and sighed. "No. I've been making turns to lose him."

"He can't track you on his phone, right?"

"Yeah, no, I turned it off."

"Good. I know Klondike. I'm heading your way."

"Thank you," she blurted, then broke down crying.

"Try to stay calm, Sunny. Keep your wits about you. I know you're scared."

"If he finds me, I'm dead, I can promise you that. I was leaving town, but I need gas. I can't do that now . . ."

"I know. I hear you. I think the best thing for tonight might be to get you to a safe house," Deetz said. "Once this blows over, you can leave town. Does that sound like a plan?"

She found herself nodding profusely. "Yes, yes." She'd do anything he said at that moment.

"Okay, good. I'm going to get the address from Callie and text it to you."

"I have it," she said. "It's in my phone someplace."

"It's the Dorcas House. Is that the one you have?"

"It's the one Callie gave me—where she volunteers."

"Right. Good. That's the one. Just to be sure we're on the same page I'll text you the address as fast as I can here in a minute."

"Okay . . ." Sunny didn't want him to end the call. He was safe. He was good.

"You're going to be fine, Sunny. Go to the Dorcas House. I'll meet you there. Okay?"

"Okay." She cried. "Thank you. Thank you so much."

"You're welcome. I'll be in touch in a minute with the address."

Instead of stopping to try to find the address for the shelter on her phone, Sunny decided to keep driving until she got the text with the address from Deetz. She approached an intersection at Austin Avenue and took a right. The rain came harder.

This is it. You're doing this.

She could feel the excitement and fear pumping through her veins.

Blaine Milligan had owned her ever since the doomed night they'd met.

She was finally fighting back.

The thought of him racing that big truck around town in search for her both made her sick with dread—and made her want to cry out laughing.

She was shivering now.

As much as she'd come to adore her little house and her job, she realized in that moment she would gladly leave them behind in exchange for her freedom.

How sick that it's had to come to this.

Her phone buzzed. It was a text from Deetz: "2404 Harmony Way."

Then the phone rang.

Blaine's sickening face blinked onto the screen.

He was calling.

Her insides shrieked in horror.

She almost sent the call to voicemail, but then paused. Dare she tell him to stop following her, that it was finally over?

It rang again.

There would be no talking to that creep. He would only scream violent threats. And for all she knew, if she answered he may have a way to track her.

She took a deep breath and sent his call to voicemail.

Take that, loser.

She needed to pull over someplace so she could put the address for Dorcas House into her map app. She drove a bit further and turned into a neighborhood. She drove back in, curved around and found a quiet cul-de-sac, where she parked the Focus.

Looking down at her left foot, she cussed when she saw that the pillowcase wrapped around it had turned blood red.

She began typing the address Deetz had sent her into her map app, when a text popped up from Blaine: "Baby I'm sorry about earlier. Come home. We can both take tomorrow off and go away someplace. Willamette Valley?"

Sunny froze, stared at the glowing screen, and read it again.

The Valley was her favorite place. Normally, she would have given in.

This was how he did it—luring her back to regain control.

How dare he, after what he'd just done to her!

Who did he think she was?

Her whole body was wounded from head to toe.

She seethed, thinking she should be in a hospital.

Did he think she was a child?

How stupid she'd been all this time with him—falling for his kiss-and-make-up stories time and time again.

Never again.

She deleted the text, flicked to the map app, and finished typing in 2404 Harmony Way. *Hmm.* Maybe she really would find 'harmony' there.

It was only a seven-minute drive.

Seven minutes to freedom.

She started the map route and braced for pain as she pushed the clutch with a grimace and took off.

17

———

Deetz was overwhelmed with fatigue and inner turmoil as he steered the Subaru through the rainy Portland night toward the Dorcas House to meet Sunny, periodically checking the glowing map on his phone as he drove. Joanie had been furious he was leaving home to work this time of night.

"A girl's life's at stake, honey," he'd insisted. "I can't not go."

Joanie had actually cried, and she wasn't a crier. Deetz knew she was just worried about him—about his health and safety, about him not getting enough sleep. The rioting in the city added to both their concerns. And she was right, the job had taken its toll, especially the last three years. Between the mass shooting at Pioneer Square, then the copycat attempt a year later, and Leena's kidnapping—he felt as if he'd aged ten years.

He sat up in his seat and squinted at himself in the rearview mirror. He flicked on the dome light. The short hair above his ears was mostly gray. His eyebrows were thinning and getting white; he preferred calling it "silver," which Joanie thought was hilarious.

Deetz still ran his three miles, three times a week, and remained at a weight with which he was happy. But, creases had etched his forehead and the corners of his eyes. His eyes looked smaller and didn't have the vibrancy they once did. There was nothing he could do about that. With each passing week the job seemed to get more difficult, physically and mentally.

He turned off the light and made a left as the map app instructed, hoping this route wasn't going to get him too close to city limits and protesting.

They had money in savings. He could retire on a reduced pension. But Leena's private school was extremely expensive. Plus, he or Joanie may eventually need long-term healthcare. And, they wanted to leave some savings to the kids. He had a little over a year to go and then he would retire with a full benefits package.

He and Joanie had always agreed they didn't want to wait until his retirement to really start living, but that's exactly what they seemed to be doing—mainly because he was so busy with work all the time.

I can't do the job halfway.

It wasn't that kind of work. He had to be all in, all the time. Peoples' lives were at stake. Some cops were lazy, he admitted it. But that wasn't in his DNA.

He checked the map on his phone; he was three minutes from the Dorcas House. He would make sure Sunny got there safely without being followed, then he would dash back home and get some shuteye. He would take care of Blaine Milligan the following day.

A good night's sleep always helped.

He turned on the radio and found the news. Another night of rioting downtown.

So much for the curfew.

Mayor Barbara Meeks had refused to get help from the federal government in the form of the National Guard. In fact, she'd basically praised the protestors and autonomous zones early on, until murder and mayhem had broken out. Now she was back peddling on her flowery love-in theme, but it was too late.

The local deejay, Jay Jones, a longtime friend of Deetz's, said there was live breaking news in the city. He sent it out to the streets . . . "This is Joshua Brandle reporting from the Multnomah County Corrections facility on Southwest Third Avenue, where protestors have tried repeatedly to set the prison on fire."

The reporter was out of breath and Deetz could hear the chaos in the background.

"Inside, Portland PD officer Wiley Fleming is being held without bond as he awaits formal charges to be filed against him in the death of twenty-seven-year-old Ronald Jacoby, the Black man who Fleming shot in an altercation several days ago after a routine traffic stop. Dozens of Portland police officers donned in full riot gear are helping put up barricades around much of the building right now, but protestors continue to set fires and throw Molotov cocktails. Members of the Portland Fire and Rescue, Precincts 13 and 27, are here to help extinguish the fires, and they've had a very busy and dangerous night on the job."

Jones next asked the reporter about the Mayor's 8 p.m. curfew.

"You wouldn't know there was a curfew," the reporter responded. "We're hours past that and there are literally hundreds of protestors here at the prison and swarming the streets of downtown Portland. Many are smashing storefront windows and looting. Portland Police are doing all they can to disperse the crowds and they are arresting the looters and agitators they can catch. Police have a number of vans here for that purpose."

Deetz clicked the radio off and whispered, "Protect our team, Lord. Keep them safe. Let this end."

Deetz's phone buzzed and a text popped on his screen from Callie Freeland. "Hi Wayne. Tyson is taking me to Dorcas House. I want to be there for Sunny. See you there."

Deetz flicked the text away and examined the map. He was within two blocks of the safe house.

He made another turn on a side street. "Let this go smoothly," he whispered. The street and surroundings looked like any other low- to middle-income city neighborhood. "Keep Blaine Milligan far from this place."

He squinted at the number on the mailbox and eased the car to a stop several hundred feet away from the average-looking, two-story Dorcas House.

The small front porch was lit by a single neon-bright LED light overhead. Several similar lights were on throughout the gray house. Deetz put the car in park and turned the lights out. "Help Sunny find freedom here. Help her start a new life."

~

CALLIE HAD RARELY SEEN Tyson so on edge. He was sitting up high in the driver's seat of his Jeep and kept looking in the rearview mirror as he drove—no doubt watching for any sign of Blaine Milligan.

Tyson's phone, which glowed from the dashboard, showed they were two minutes from the Dorcas House.

The periodic swish of windshield wipers was the only sound inside the vehicle besides the occasional verbal instruction from the map app on his phone.

Callie sat there numb and tired as they rode in the rainy night.

Both of their minds had been blown that day by the actions of Blaine Milligan—from his confrontation with Deetz that morning to the text message and Friend request he'd brashly sent to Callie. Then the gasoline antic at her apartment.

Her head reeled from it all.

And to think he'd actually found out where she worked, drove around the security gate, watched her, shot that gun—it was *insanity*.

"I'm sorry about all this," she said.

Tyson glanced over at her in the dark car then looked back at the road. "It's not your fault, Freeland. You're just trying to help a friend."

"I pick some real winners," she said.

"Ha. That's true. Then again, you picked me," Tyson said.

They both chuckled softly, which felt good amid the tension.

"Thanks for doing this," Callie said.

"You're welcome. We'll make sure she gets there okay, then we'll hunker down for the night. I may take tomorrow off."

"Why?"

"I'm not leaving you with that freak on the loose."

"I'll be fine. He doesn't know where you live."

"He can find it; he's proven that."

"Deetz is going to arrest him."

Tyson nodded. "Fine. When he does, I'll go back to work. I'm not letting anything happen to you."

They rode on in silence.

That had been a reference to Tyson's wife, Kim, who'd died in the Portland shooting several years ago.

The female voice from Tyson's phone prompted him and he made a left onto Harmony Way, again checking his rearview mirror. The street name struck Callie each time she volunteered at the Dorcas House. It was indeed a place—a hideaway—where women from all walks of life sought safety, peace, shelter, security, and, yes, the beginning of some sort of harmony in their lives.

Dorcas, Callie had learned when she started volunteering there, was a woman from the Bible who was known for her good works and acts of charity. Also known as Tabitha, she was said to be a widow and was part of the inner circle of the early church.

"Is this right?" Tyson broke the silence, looking around at the homes. "This is a regular neighborhood."

"Yeah, just stay on this. It'll wind around to it."

"How big is it? Is it just a house? How many women can it hold?"

"Sixteen max."

"Sixteen? Wow."

"It's four bedrooms up, two to a room. Huge finished basement has four more bedrooms, two to a room. But I've never seen more than eight or ten there at a time. Usually, they get their own room."

"What if they have kids?"

"The kids take up those spaces. They make it work."

Tyson pulled the Jeep off to the side of the road about a quarter-mile from the house, stopped, and parked.

"What are you doing?" Callie said.

Tyson looked behind them and down the road in front of them. "Just want to make sure he's not following."

"Good call."

"No more word from Sunny? I guess that's good," Tyson said.

Callie nodded.

The car was silent.

Callie spoke softly, "Jesus, let her get here safely. Protect her. Protect us all."

"Amen to that." Tyson looked all around once more, put the Jeep in drive and eased back onto the quiet street. Around the next corner his phone announced they had reached their destination.

"That's Deetz's car," Callie said, feeling her heart rate increase.

Tyson eased up behind the Subaru, put the Jeep in park, and turned it off.

Callie could see Deetz's head inside the dark car. It gave her a sense of relief he'd been there awhile scoping out the situation.

Her phone buzzed. It was a text from Deetz: "Where will Sunny park?"

"Oh, that's right," Callie said, tapping away at her phone. "I need to tell Sunny to park in back." She texted Deetz and Sunny about the driveway that led around to the rear of the house.

"She should be getting here, shouldn't she?" Tyson said.

Callie checked the time. He was right, she was due.

"Yeah . . . Come on, Sunny."

Callie tried to stay positive, tried to tell herself Sunny would make it safely. But, in the time she'd known Sunny, there'd been no denying that bad luck and trouble followed her like a shadow.

Callie envisioned Sunny flying up to the Dorcas House in her little Ford—with Blaine Milligan right on her tail.

"Heads up." Tyson adjusted his rearview mirror. "Here comes a car."

18

———

Sunny's heart rate hummed as she drove the outskirts of the city, getting closer to the Dorcas House.

The text from Callie said to park in back of the shelter.

Three more minutes . . .

She checked the rearview mirror. Still no sign of Blaine.

A steady rain fell. She had the windows cracked, refreshed by the cold night air and mist from the rain.

She wasn't familiar with the street she was on and simply trusted the map app to guide her, as always.

Hopeful thoughts filled her head about where she might go, what she might do after this night. She'd always heard Virginia was beautiful and had even researched it quite often, without Blaine knowing, of course. She'd zeroed in on Virginia Beach and Richmond, both of which looked like vibrant mid-size cities, close to the beach, with good employment opportunities.

She pictured herself laying on a thick white towel beneath a royal blue umbrella on the golden sand, enjoying the Atlantic breeze and the relaxing sound of the waves crashing against the shoreline.

She hadn't been this excited since she put the down payment on her house.

She didn't care what kind of job she had to get at first, or where she had to live—she could survive anything after what she'd been

93

through. It would all be like a vacation compared to life as it had been under Blaine's rule.

"Turn left on Andover Boulevard." The voice from the map app drew her back to reality.

She made the turn and made sure he was nowhere in sight.

With each passing block, she felt a new and positive energy.

Brake lights shone in the misty night ahead. As she slowed down it dawned on her, she'd not only been under Blaine's authority when he'd been with her, but she'd been living in a constant state of horror around the clock, each hour, each minute—never sure what he would say or do next. The threatening text messages and bizarre calls—stating that he was watching her, that he knew what she was doing every second of the day. The door to her house unlocking in the middle of the night and him . . . creeping into bed next to her.

She began to cry and laugh at the same time.

You're doing this. You're going to be free!

Chills raced up and down her entire body. She shivered.

Just as she found the buttons to put the windows up, she noticed three or four vehicles stopped ahead of her, but the traffic light was green.

With pain searing as she pushed the clutch, she shifted into neutral and glided toward the stopped cars.

People filled the streets.

"Uh oh."

She reached up and adjusted the rearview mirror, her hand trembling.

A small car eased to a stop behind her.

She looked around for options, for a way out, but there were no more streets between her car and the traffic light ahead, which was about a hundred yards away.

Protestors filled the intersection like fans at a sporting event.

Some were drifting toward her.

The crowd was spreading.

Cars heading toward her, on the opposite side of the blocked intersection, were stopped as well, stacking up behind the protestors.

Again, she looked around urgently.

The only way out would be to make a U-turn and let the map app readjust and tell her a different way to get to the shelter.

Should I?

She checked back again. Several more cars had stopped behind her.

Ahead, no cars were able to come toward her through the intersection; it was completely blocked by the thickening crowd. Some carried signs. Some wore masks to cover their identities. She saw no police. It was chaos.

The car in front of her abruptly lurched forward, turned around, and jetted away.

Sunny rolled the Ford forward on the slight incline.

Then she saw him.

Straight ahead. Across the intersection. Sitting high up in his monster truck.

She gasped.

But she got hold of herself.

He can't get through. Calm down!

The crowd was too large.

Right?

Right? He can't get through.

But no, wait . . . no!

Blaine's truck was bumping forward, forging into the intersection, into the crowd!

Of course he was—because that's what Blaine Milligan did.

Sunny was paralyzed . . . watching, hearing his truck rev and inch forward, slowly but steadily moving ahead—forcing people out of his way.

But the protestors were catching on to what he was doing. They started to yell and wave others over! They were swarming Blaine's truck, beginning to rock it.

Sunny couldn't move.

Deep in the recesses of her mind a voice was telling her to go.

Leave.

Get out!

But she wanted to see them hurt him, tip over the truck, burn it.

She stared in awe with her mouth gaping open, still thinking he could not possibly get through.

But the truck roared so loudly it shook. He must've put it in neutral and floored it. Some of the people jumped away, but others were not daunted. More joined in. Several hopped into the bed of the truck.

He'll be furious!

"Be careful, people. You don't know who you're dealing with," she whispered.

Suddenly the truck lurched forward four feet and buckled to a stop.

People scrambled away, falling, screaming.

The truck jumped forward again another three feet and jerked to a halt, sending more people scrambling.

Crazy nutcase.

Chills swept over Sunny.

Get out!

She jammed the clutch with her hurt foot, found first gear, and revved the little car forward and swung it around to her left.

But she was forced to stop almost immediately, because other cars had done the same thing—turned around.

"No!"

Sunny pounded the wheel and craned her head back toward the intersection. Blaine's truck was inching closer to freedom on Sunny's side of the crowd.

She turned back and laid on her horn. Others were chiming in.

The cars in front of her began to move and she goosed the Ford forward, not allowing others to U-turn in front of her.

"Go, go, go!" she screamed and turned back to look.

Blaine's truck jerked to a stop again in the crowd. More people had jumped into the back. His window went down. His arm stuck out . . .

A blaze of thundering white gunfire ripped across the night sky.

"Oh my gosh . . ."

People dove and fell and screamed and scurried.

Bodies parted like the Red Sea.

The road was wide open in front of him.

He would be on her in an instant.

Sunny screamed and turned back to the road in front of her.

The cars had cleared.

Cars honked from behind.

Unable to breathe, she frantically grabbed the shift, gassed the car, and jetted forward, pain piercing her left foot.

She looked at the map on her phone and cursed—it was recalculating her route and temporarily didn't give her a current view.

"Come on, come on!" she yelled, looking in her rearview.

Blaine had fallen in line with the cars behind her.

He was only four cars back.

She shifted and floored it and repeated as fast as she could, getting the Focus up to cruising speed.

"Turn right on Howard Street."

Finally.

She glanced at the map to make sure she was at the right intersection, then dove off onto Howard Street, flying over a steep incline, her stomach flipping like she was on a rollercoaster.

She turned back, horrified to see Blaine's truck in the wrong lane, roaring past the other cars.

She floored it, knowing she was driving way too fast on the wet pavement, but choosing that over the alternative of being caught.

She clicked on her bright lights.

If she continued to the Dorcas House, she would lead Blaine right to it.

But the cop was there, and Tyson and Callie. They would help her.

In her rearview mirror, Blaine's truck made the same turn, took the dip and hugged the incline like a magnet—roaring toward her as if he'd just hit an afterburner.

19

THE INTERIOR of Deetz's Subaru was completely silent. Tyson had pulled in behind him with Callie a little while ago. They were waiting on Sunny to arrive.

One car passed a minute ago, but that was the only vehicle so far.

A light went out in the Dorcas House.

Deetz put his window down a crack, amazed at the stillness and quietness of the neighborhood.

He kept thinking about the protests, his kids, how the country had changed, and how insane it was that a growing segment of the population actually wanted to do away with police. The cities doing so were quickly going to hell in a handbasket—like his own.

Within the past few years the country had become starkly divided on many issues, and that troubled Deetz at his core. There was so much hatred and blame coming from both sides. It seemed everyone had a boiling opinion about everything, and anyone who didn't agree was considered the enemy. Long gone were the days of talking about matters until a fair agreement was reached.

Joanie seemed to be able to watch the news and not get caught up in it, but not Deetz. It made him steam. She told him not to watch.

Deetz put his window down the rest of the way. It had almost stopped raining. He closed his eyes and relished the silence. Crickets chirped. A bit of peace for a few moments.

He was disappointed in himself for getting caught up in the emotional swirl of the political wars, the rioting, the social justice movement, the cancel culture. He knew in his heart that his hope was not in man and not in one political party or another, it was in God. But it was so easy to read the feeds and opinions on social media and to get all worked up and negative.

Where he found peace was reading his Bible for a few minutes each morning. That clear truth never failed to recalibrate his mind and rejuvenate his soul.

"Hey Detective." Tyson's voice surprised him. "Past your bedtime, isn't it?"

Deetz chuckled. "Been a heck of a day, hasn't it? I'm surprised Sunny's not here yet."

"I know." Tyson rested a hand on Deetz's car. "We're wondering if something went wrong."

"Have you guys tried to contact her lately?" Deetz said.

"No. You think we should?"

"Why don't I call her real quick," Deetz said.

Just then, headlight beams from a car swept across the trees.

"That might be her. I'm gonna jump back in with Callie." Tyson hurried back to the Jeep.

Deetz turned back and watched the car approach.

The vehicle was low and small and looked like it may be Sunny's Focus.

He got out of his car and watched.

It was coming fast.

Too fast.

Something wasn't right.

Deetz squinted into the night with his eyes fixed on the road behind Sunny's car.

He waited, hoping he was wrong.

But the trees gradually lit up again.

A huge truck squealed as it hugged the corner, its bright lights bouncing as it headed toward them.

It's him.

Deetz took a deep breath, unholstered his gun, and racked the slide. For a half-second, he was light-headed and felt off balance.

As Sunny's headlights hit him, he waved for her to stop, which she did right beside him. Her passenger window went down and she was frantic. "He's coming. I'm sorry! I didn't know what else to do. I didn't mean to bring him here."

Tyson and Callie started to get out of the Jeep.

"Stop. Get back in, guys," Deetz said. "He's coming right now. Get in, lock your doors. Tyson, if you have your Sig, get it ready, just in case."

"What the heck do I do?" Sunny screamed.

"Pull in front of my car," Deetz ordered. "Stay inside. Keep the doors locked. Hurry."

"I'm sorry," Sunny said again as the Focus lurched forward, turned, and parked at an awkward angle in front of Deetz's Subaru.

Blaine Milligan's truck roared straight at them.

Deetz positioned himself between his car and Tyson's. He squared up, legs spread apart with the Glock locked, loaded, and trained on Milligan's neon bright headlights rocketing toward him.

Deetz stood square in Milligan's headlights now.

He sees me . . .

His heart thundered. After almost thirty-five years on the job, the buzz of the chase, the takedown, it never changed. It was like putting fear, adrenaline, and uncertainty into a blender and flipping the switch.

Deetz would arrest him now and worry about evidence tomorrow.

When it was forty yards away, Milligan's truck slowed.

The ground seemed to shift.

Something didn't feel right.

Milligan's truck rumbled back to life, coming straight at Deetz.

When the truck was within earshot, Deetz yelled, "Stop, police!" He was ready to fire into the cab if he had to.

The truck came in hot but skidded to a halt ten yards from Deetz.

"Park and get out," Deetz yelled. "You're under arrest."

The bright lights made it impossible to see.

Deetz heard three loud electronic clicks and immediately knew Milligan had a PA system built into the truck.

"Get out of the way—Ditz." Milligan's voice boomed from an exterior speaker. "This ain't none of your business, now move."

Deetz glanced into Tyson's Jeep and saw him holding up his gun to show he was ready.

"I'm arresting you for stalking and threats, breaking and entering, and credit card theft," Deetz yelled above the loud idling of the truck engine. "Get out of the vehicle, *now.*"

The truck suddenly roared so loudly it hurt Deetz's ears as it reverberated in place, sending a wave of heat drifting past Deetz.

"Sunny," Milligan's blaring voice boomed over the redneck PA system, "You get into this truck right now or someone's gonna die. You know I mean it." Then his blaring horn sounded for five seconds. "Now!"

Sunny's car door opened.

"No, Sunny!" Deetz yelled. "Stay in. Keep it locked!"

"He'll kill you!" Sunny yelled at Deetz. "He's not right. He'll do it."

Milligan's truck shifted and lurched forward like an enormous robot.

Deetz took aim and fired.

Milligan's large left headlight exploded with a bright flash and went black. He stopped.

Sunny screamed.

Deetz was temporarily blinded by the neon spot from the headlight in his vision.

Sunny's door closed and Deetz could hear Tyson and Callie arguing about what to do.

Milligan screamed a string of expletives over the loudspeaker.

"Get out now, Milligan," Deetz yelled, his heart pounding. "You're under arrest. I'm not asking again."

Deetz felt weak, but he knew he had to finish this.

Milligan cussed over the PA system and the truck spit gravel and heaved toward Deetz.

Deetz dove out of the way and rolled into wet cinders and weeds. He got to his knees just in time to see the truck fishtail and crunch the side of his car, then continue swinging around toward the way it'd come in.

Tyson opened his door to get out.

"Stay in!" Deetz yelled, then took aim at Milligan's tires and fired repeatedly. Two or three shots hit the truck. He couldn't tell if he'd hit any of the tires.

Smelling fuel from the truck in the damp air, Deetz watched from the ground as the truck's tires squealed and it roared into the night in a cloud of white smoke. Just before it went out of sight around the corner, the loudspeaker clicked. "Joanie's next. Hear me? Joanie's next!"

20

———

Once she realized Blaine was gone, all Sunny had the wherewithal to do was sit in her car and cry.

When will this end?

She was completely spent.

Her head dropped to her chest and she sobbed.

Her whole body hurt; her left foot felt as if it had broken off.

Where will he go now?

There was a knock at her window. It was Callie's fiancé, Tyson. She put the window down and looked up at him.

"You okay?" he said.

She nodded and tried to hold back the tears. "Sorry to drag you into this." She cursed.

"Sunny, Wayne's not doing well. He thinks it's a panic attack or something."

Sunny opened her door.

"You don't have to get out. Callie's with him," Tyson said. "We're trying to figure out what to do next. You can't stay here now."

Sunny looked back without getting out of the car but couldn't see Deetz. "Where is he?"

Tyson looked back. "On the ground, leaning against my Jeep. Trying to regroup. He's had these attacks before. He says he'll be fine."

"Callie's with him?"

"Yeah."

"I'd get out, but my foot is hurt really bad," Sunny said.

"What happened?"

She looked up at him. "Blaine."

Tyson arched his back and sighed. "We need to figure out what to do. You obviously can't go home. We're thinking maybe you should stay with us tonight at my place, but I can't guarantee he won't show up there. He's threatened Callie."

Sunny slumped back in her seat.

She wanted to disappear.

You're nothing but a burden . . . endangering these peoples' lives.

"Your head's bleeding." Tyson nodded toward her scalp, where Blaine had yanked hair from her head.

"I'm fine." Sunny reached between the seats, pulled out a tissue and wiped her eyes and nose. "How bad is Deetz's car?"

"Both doors got swiped. He'll have to get in the passenger door, but it's drivable."

"I think I'm gonna just get out of Dodge," Sunny said.

"Now?" Tyson looked at his watch. "It's almost midnight."

"He's probably watching us right now, somehow. I don't want you guys to get hurt."

"He's long gone," Tyson said.

"You don't know him. He's watching, somehow."

Tyson sighed again.

He thinks I'm nuts.

"I'm just trying to figure out the safest thing for you, for everybody," Tyson said.

Sunny cringed. She was a parasite.

"Look, I'm going," she said.

"You're not heading out in the middle of the night," Deetz yelled from the darkness.

Then Sunny heard Deetz ask Callie to help him up.

A few seconds later, they both showed up at Sunny's car.

"I'm so sorry," Sunny addressed Deetz and Callie. "Are you okay?"

Deetz nodded. "What about you?"

Sunny nodded.

"I'm so sorry. All of you have been so kind," Sunny said. "He's on a suicide mission. I really believe that. He's a miserable person. He hates his life. I honestly believe he wants to die."

Sunny broke down again.

"That's fine, but it looks like he wants you to die with him," Deetz said. "That is not okay and it's not going to happen."

Deetz reached out his hands and leaned against Sunny's car.

"You sure you're okay?" Callie said.

With his head down, looking at the ground, Deetz inhaled deeply, exhaled, and did it again.

"Yeah. I'm good. This hasn't happened in a long time." He shook his head.

"What do you want to do, Wayne?" Tyson said.

Deetz stood up straight. "I need to get home to Joanie."

Sunny said, "You need to warn her—"

"I did," Deetz said. "She's locked in, and armed. But I need to get home. If you guys are still good with it, let's have Sunny stay with you tonight. I'll arrange for at least one officer to be there overnight. If you're good with that I'll call it in and have them meet you at your place, Tyson."

Tyson and Callie nodded.

"I'm putting out an APB for Milligan."

"Now?" Sunny said.

"Yes. And we'll keep your house under surveillance around the clock. I want this guy."

Sunny nodded and grabbed another tissue.

"What about Sunny's car?" Tyson said. "He'll see it at my place."

Deetz nodded and paused.

"How about if we park it here overnight?" Deetz nodded toward the Dorcas House. "Park it in back. You guys drive Sunny to your place."

"I'm afraid what he'll do—tonight," Sunny said.

"I think we're gonna be okay," Deetz said. "Hopefully our guys may get him tonight." He addressed Sunny. "You don't know where else he may be staying? Or, where else he may go?"

Sunny shook her head. "He had a place in Oatfield. I don't think he still does; he couldn't afford it. I don't know where he stays when he's not with me. I know he goes to the American Legion post to drink, but other than that, he tells me nothing."

"Okay," Deetz said. "I'm praying for protection for all of us tonight. And that this guy is brought to justice—even overnight."

Callie and Tyson nodded in agreement.

Even Sunny found herself whispering, "Amen to that."

21

AMAZINGLY, the remainder of the anxiety-filled night was uneventful. It was as if Blaine Milligan had vanished. Either that, or he seemed to be a long way from Portland, Oregon.

Armed with two guns, Deetz had sat up all night in an uncomfortable chair in the dark of his living room, watching and listening for any sign of Milligan while Joanie and Leena slept. Tyson Cooper had done the same at his place, keeping vigilant watch over Callie and Sunny with his dependable Sig Sauer at his side.

But nothing ever happened.

As Deetz stood in a tired daze in front of the humming microwave in the breakroom at Portland PD headquarters, he reflected on what he'd done already that morning and what he still had to do. He was warming his last cup of coffee. It was 11:15 a.m.

Faithful Joanie had gotten up with him to get him off to work with his thermos and lunch, as usual. Even though she'd been upset about Deetz leaving so late the night before and worried about Blaine Milligan's intrusion in their lives, she'd arisen with a smile and a hug for Deetz, and had even remembered to have him tear off the next loop in the colorful paper chain she'd created. Each ring of paper represented one less day until his retirement; that morning he'd torn off number four hundred and thirteen.

The days can't go fast enough.

Deetz retrieved his coffee and made a beeline for his cubicle, dodging Virgil and Wesley because he was cranky from lack of sleep and had way too much to do.

Seated at his desk, he got his notes out and opened his laptop. The APB had turned up nothing overnight or that morning. And there had been no sign of Milligan at Sunny's house, according to the cops stationed in their car across the street from her place. Deetz found the address where Milligan worked and sent it to his printer.

Earlier that morning, Deetz had advised Sunny to take the day off of work and to stay with Callie. Tyson had called into his school and taken the day off as well. Sunny had phoned Deetz at 10:45 a.m. and told him she, Callie and Tyson were going to her house to straighten the place up and get a few more things she'd forgotten; she said she'd left the house in complete disarray the day before and wanted to get it organized. Deetz was okay with that, because the house was under surveillance and Tyson and Callie would be with her.

Everyone was waiting for Milligan to resurface so an arrest could be made and people could resume their lives, but thus far the creep had done a good job of going dark since his antics the night before.

Deetz had stopped at the local American Legion post that morning and showed Milligan's photo to five men who sat around drinking McDonald's coffee. Only one said he'd seen Milligan in there before, and it had been months ago.

Deetz had spent thirty minutes on the phone with the head of security at Callie's warehouse and with the manager at her apartment complex. Both had confirmed, based on photos Deetz sent them of Milligan, that it was indeed Milligan who was stalking Callie at the warehouse and dousing her apartment hallway with gasoline. Deetz was attempting to have them make the video footage accessible to him online either via email or cloud. They were both working on it. If they couldn't do it, Deetz would have to go in person.

Deetz reviewed the hand-written list of charges he intended to bring against Blaine Milligan: felony domestic violence, felony assault, credit card theft, breaking and entering at Callie's warehouse, attempted arson, threatening, stalking, and menacing. He was sure others would surface as they found out more about Milligan's recent activity.

He looked at his watch. Almost 11:30 a.m. The day had flown past. He badly wanted to arrest Milligan before dark. None of them wanted to spend another night on pins and needles, wondering if the nutjob was going to surface again—and what he might do next.

Deetz stood up, yawned, and stretched. His right knee hurt from when he dove out of Milligan's way the night before. He examined a scrape on the palm of his left hand. He thought about his car—where and when he would find the time to get it repaired.

I'm so done with this.

He was disappointed about the anxiety flare-ups he'd experienced within the last day. That was a setback. He thought those were a thing of the past. He hadn't told Joanie; she had enough to worry about.

He grabbed the printout with Milligan's work address, got his jacket, and headed for his car.

His phone buzzed on the way. It was a call back from the Oatfield Police Department.

"Deetz," he answered.

"Hey, Deetz, this is Sebastian calling from Oatfield PD."

"Thanks for getting back so quickly," Deetz said.

"No problem. Listen, I checked out that address for Blaine Milligan myself and the tenants who live there now have been in there for two-and-a-half months, so he's long gone."

"Okay. That helps me. Thank you. Tell me, Sebastian, what kind of place was it?"

"Extended stay hotel. Cheap and rundown. Way on the outskirts of town."

Deetz thanked him again and ended the call. He got into his car via the passenger door and sat on that side while he tapped the address for Milligan's employer into his phone. The map app said it was a fifteen minute drive.

He was about to crawl over to the driver's seat when he felt as if he was shoved by a wave of anxiety.

His head spun.

He put his hands on the dashboard.

"No," he whispered.

It took his breath away.

He got out of the car and took in a giant breath of air, held it, then exhaled. Then he did it again. He looked around to see if anyone was watching. They were not.

He paced and wiped the sweat from his forehead.

It was in the fifties and he was sweating.

He was so frustrated at himself.

What is wrong with you?

"Why does this happen?" he mumbled.

He'd been through all the tests after the trauma of the original Portland mass shooting. They'd called it "panic disorder." He'd been through weeks of "talk therapy" with a Christian counselor.

Remembering the counselor's advice that had helped him most, Deetz plopped down in the front passenger seat with the door open and one foot outside, put his head back and closed his eyes. He took in a deep breath and focused on relaxing from head to feet. The breathing and relaxation techniques had been part of his treatment, along with exercise—which he did faithfully.

With his eyes closed and a cool breeze blowing into the car, Deetz silently recited Jesus's words from the scripture that had helped him keep his sanity: *Peace I leave with you, my peace I give you. I do not give to you as the world gives. Do not let your heart be troubled and do not be afraid.*

He forced himself to feed on those words.

He's given you supernatural peace. He's here. He's in you.

Deetz shook his head.

What am I so worried about? What's triggering this?

He'd been trained to ask himself that.

His mind went back to the heated showdown in front of Sunny's house the morning before. The red gas can and sickening, heavy smell of fuel. The roaring truck, strange PA system, and shots fired the night before.

Blaine Milligan's causing this.

Then, Blaine Milligan needs to come down.

22

———

L ATE MORNING DAYLIGHT flooded Sunny's little house and Callie was shocked seeing the blood on the carpet throughout, and the blood and hair on her messed up bed. Several times she looked questioningly at Sunny—as if to ask how she could have lived like that for so long—but each time Sunny quickly looked away and got busy with other things.

Tyson appeared with a rag in his hand at the doorway of Sunny's bedroom. He'd come from the front room where he was attempting to spot clean the carpet.

"We should probably get your car, put it in your garage," Tyson said.

"That would be good," Sunny said, as she and Callie stripped the bed of its crimson spotted sheets. "For sure. I need my wheels."

Callie noticed Sunny was still limping. They'd cleaned and bandaged her foot at Tyson's place the night before and put antibiotic ointment on it and on her scalp where Blaine Milligan had removed a fist full of her hair.

"To be honest, guys, I'm thinking of taking my chances and hitting the road," Sunny said. "If we can get my car and gas, that's all I need. I'm out."

Callie looked at Tyson.

"They're going to get him, Sunny," Tyson said. "Just wait with us. You're safe now. You won't be safe if you go out on the road by yourself. You said yourself he's always watching you."

"If you guys can just help me get gas and make sure he's not following me, see me out of town, I'll be fine," Sunny said. "I want to get out of here, far from here."

"Sunny, this is all going to end, probably today," Callie said. "When they arrest him, you get to keep your house, keep your job, get your life back. These are felony charges we're talking about. He's going to go away for a long time."

Sunny stuck her hands on her waist and shook her head. "If you only knew this guy . . . He's not gonna get caught. If I stay in Portland, he's gonna find me. Guaranteed. And in the meantime, your lives are at risk. You and Deetz, and his family."

"There's another shelter," Callie said. "Winchester Place. If they don't arrest him by late afternoon, I say we take you there. It's in the city. Another generic neighborhood, a lot like Dorcas House. He won't find you there—I promise you."

Sunny had begun objecting before Callie finished talking.

"I've already endangered your lives and Deetz's. I'm not about to endanger the lives of the ladies at that place," Sunny said.

In silence, Callie and Sunny made the bed up with fresh sheets, pillowcases, and blanket. Tyson went to one of the two windows and peered through the slats.

"Police still there?" Callie asked.

"Yep," he said.

"One cop ain't gonna stop him," Sunny said. "I'm serious. I need to get out of town. We're done here. Let's at least get my car."

"I was going to vacuum," Callie said.

"Don't worry about it," Sunny said.

"How about I stay and vacuum and you guys get the car and come back?" Callie said.

Tyson craned his neck toward her in exaggeration. "Are you serious? No way."

"He's right," Sunny said. "You can't stay here alone."

"Okay, okay," Callie said. "I just want to get this place all in order for when you come back."

"Let's do this," Tyson said. "We'll take a break, grab a bite, and get the car. You can vacuum when we come back, and I've got a few more spots to try to clean. That'll be it."

"By then, they'll have him," Callie says.

"Let's hope so," Tyson said.

"Don't count on it," Sunny said.

AFTER DEETZ HAD DRIVEN AROUND FOREVER within the massive Stratton & Katz Lumber Company complex, he finally found the small office the guard at the gate had told him about. He parked and approached the log cabin style building. The screen door squeaked when he opened it and slammed like a mousetrap behind him.

"What can we do you for?" said a large man swiveling in his chair behind a small desk.

Deetz held out his badge and introduced himself as Portland PD. "I'm looking for Blaine Milligan. Heard he works here. Can you help me?"

"Oh boy," the large man stood up, nearly knocking over the little chair. "I'm Ronnie. Ronnie Gerard. I know Milligan, but I don't think he's been around for a few days. Let me check the schedule."

Deetz thanked him as he crossed to another desk, leaned over and clicked the mouse and space bar to wake up the old computer sitting there. "He in some kind of trouble?" Ronnie said.

"I can't say. It's just imperative I find him as fast as possible."

"Well, let's see here then." Ronnie clicked and scrolled. It took some time. He scrolled more. "Okay, here we go. Looks like he's out sick; has been the last two days."

"When's he due to work next?" Deetz said.

Ronnie moved the mouse and examined the screen. "He's off tomorrow, then works three days in a row after that."

"Is he full time?"

"Yep."

"How long's he worked here?"

The man straightened up from the computer. "Now you're asking me things I don't know how to find," he said. "I can get that answer for you when Sally gets back from lunch. She's our office manager."

"Is he a good employee?" Deetz said.

Ronnie put his hands out and shook his head. "I'm not sure, sir. We employ like seventy-five people. I've not heard anything negative. Again, Sally will be back soon. But I can tell you, we don't keep bad apples."

"I suppose I'd need to get his most recent home address and phone number from Sally?" Deetz was hoping Milligan had another place of residence or phone number they hadn't found out about yet.

Ronnie held out a hand toward the computer. "Yeah, sorry, I don't know how to access that stuff. She'll probably be back in thirty minutes."

Deetz dug in his coat pocket and held out a business card with his phone number on it.

Ronnie took it with a huge hand.

"Will you have her call me when she gets back?" Deetz said.

"Sure will," Ronnie said, and began walking to the door with Deetz.

Just then, the phone in Deetz's pocket vibrated and gave off a loud, obnoxious intermittent buzzing tone. That only happened when it was an important text alert from Portland PD headquarters.

Deetz grabbed the phone, thanked Ronnie, and exited the office, the door snapping shut behind him.

As a stiff, cold wind blew, he stopped halfway between the office and his car to read the message: "Portland PD ALERT: While being transported to court, Officer Wiley Fleming was shot outside Multnomah County Courthouse and is being transported to Sisters of Charity Hospital. Condition serious. Shooter at large. Description: white male approximately 25, 6-foot, 160 pounds, long red hair, last seen wearing white hoodie, royal blue sweatpants, white tennis shoes, Dodgers' bandana. Last seen fleeing east on SW Salmon St but may have been picked up in a gray Dodge Challenger. More information to come."

· · ·

Deetz hurried to his car, got in the passenger side, climbed over to his seat, and sat there. His pulse pounded at his temples. He gathered himself, taking deep breaths.

Now he had two major events breaking at once—the pursuit of Blaine Milligan, and a potential civil war on his streets.

Thus far, the conservative right had been mostly silent. But now, Wiley Fleming, a white cop, had been shot, likely by the group protesting for racial justice and police defunding. Deetz was afraid if Mayor Barbara Meeks didn't ask the federal government to send in the National Guard, there could be major bloodshed.

Deetz had been keeping his eye on a radical right conservative group known as the Portland Patriots, which had met several times over the past week at various city parks, hundreds of them carrying rifles and donning helmets and body armor. The liberal media called them white supremacists, while the conservative media labeled them freedom fighters who'd had it with the uprising, looting, and bloodshed on their streets.

Deetz found himself sweating and lightheaded, fidgeting with his fingers and then his phone.

Stop.

Calm down, man.

He gripped the steering wheel with both hands and made himself get still. Made himself relax his body and mind as much as he could.

Breathe.

He thought of calling Joanie or his therapist.

He lowered his head and whispered one of the few things from the Bible he'd ever memorized. "Blessed is the man who trusts in the Lord . . . whose confidence is in Him."

I can't do this.

Help me.

He continued, picturing the words in his mind. "He'll be like a tree planted by the water, that sends it roots out by the stream . . . It has no fear when heat comes, its leaves are always green. It has no worry in a year of drought, and never fails to bear fruit."

He was cold.

He blew warm air into his cupped hands repeatedly.

There in the car, he soaked in the silence and tried to be still for another moment; just feeling God's presence.

Because, he knew, things were about to get crazy.

23

———

Sunny rode in the backseat of Tyson's Jeep, eyes peeled for Blaine Milligan's dreaded truck. Tyson was driving and Callie was up front, taking Sunny to get her car where she'd left it the night before—behind the Dorcas House.

The sun was out. It was one of those crisp, crystal clear, green and blue fall days in the Pacific Northwest. Too bad Sunny didn't live a normal life so she could enjoy it. Her body hurt all over— wrists, scalp, left foot, the arm that got mangled behind her back— but she'd been forced to live with such pain. In a weird way, it made her feel like a survivor.

Sunny flicked through her phone as they rode. She wasn't going to tell Callie and Tyson, but she really did want to go to the other shelter, Winchester Place. Ideally, she could stay there for a few days until Blaine was arrested, like Callie and Tyson had suggested, then she could move back into her house, keep her job.

But she was afraid Blaine would track her down, endanger other lives at the shelter, possibly even hurt Callie.

I've got to get out of here. Far away. For their sakes.

As they rode, Tyson and Callie talked quietly up front, some- thing about a family reunion coming up.

Sunny had purposefully not listened to the voicemail Blaine left the night before. She knew he would either be pleading innocently

117

for her to come back, or it would be a blistering stream of profanity and threats.

She tapped to voicemail, put the phone to her ear, and played Blaine's message. "Sunny, baby, I'm sorry. I'm so sorry. Don't do this. Don't run. Please. You know I'll find you anyway. Look, let me make it up to you. Come home. Get yourself a warm bath. Burn some candles. Relax. We can both take tomorrow off and just get away. Who cares where? Just be alone. Please, baby, you know I love you. Let me prove it to you. Okay, see you soon . . . Sunny, you get me? One way or another, I *will* see you soon."

Click. The recording ended and chills swept up and down her spine. Even when he set out to play nice, the message was laced with underlying bossiness and intimidation.

Although she actually considered it momentarily, Sunny knew if she went back this time, he'd kill her.

She needed a new phone. She decided when she stopped to get gas in the Focus, she'd buy a burner phone—that's what they called it on the shows she watched. She would pitch hers, or keep it for back up.

Then it dawned on her—she could turn on location services on her current phone and leave it on a bus or something—send Blaine on a wild goose chase while she snuck out of town.

It could work.

Sunny realized Callie was talking to her.

"I'm sorry, what?" Sunny said.

"What do you want to eat?" Callie pointed outside.

They were sitting at a McDonald's drive-thru and Sunny hadn't even noticed.

"Oh my gosh, I'm sorry, I was in a daze," Sunny said. "Fish sandwich and a large Coke. That's it."

Tyson ordered for everyone.

Sunny dug five bucks out of her purse and handed it to Callie, who assured her it was their treat. She tucked the money in the door handle and looked back at her phone. She remembered when Blaine had bought it for her. He'd done so because he'd smashed her other one on her kitchen floor in a jealous rage. That was another time he'd choked her neck so tightly that she'd actually flickered in and out of consciousness.

She took the sandwich and drink Callie handed her and perked up in her seat.

This is a new day. Putting the past behind.

The sandwich and drink tasted so good. She was starved.

The more Sunny thought about her phone, the more anxious she felt that Blaine hadn't been calling and texting her. That creeped her out. She turned around and looked at the cars behind them for his truck. She scanned all around. He was nowhere in sight.

"Any word from Deetz?" she said.

"Nada," Tyson said.

"Hopefully soon," Callie said.

Sunny had come to love and appreciate Callie, Tyson, and Deetz —but they were so naïve. They thought this was going to be easy. Put an APB out and bring the guy in.

But Blaine Milligan played by no one's rules. He was a *rulebreaker.* He took normal and flipped it on its can. He never failed to do the unexpected. Just when Sunny thought she could put her guard down, Blaine would explode into a rage about something, anything, always completely unexpected—filling Sunny with terror.

He was in and out of doctor's offices and therapy sessions, and on and off the medications they would prescribe.

How did I let him into my life? It makes me look so stupid.

As she did so often, Sunny felt like a downright fool—not only for opening a door for Blaine to enter her life, but for allowing him to have complete reign over her for so long.

Can it be over?

Could last night have been the last time Blaine would ever abuse her? The last time *anyone* would ever abuse her?

The thought of such freedom gave Sunny chills. Tears flooded her eyes. She grabbed her napkin and wiped them.

"You're quiet back there," Tyson said.

Sunny was so choked up, she couldn't speak. She tried but only ended up laughing.

Callie turned around to look at her. "Aww. You okay?"

Sunny nodded. "Yeah."

"Here." Callie handed her several tissues.

"Thanks." Sunny took them and wiped her eyes and nose.

"You've been through so much," Callie said.

Tyson looked at Sunny in the rearview mirror.

"I'm just . . ." Sunny cried. ". . . I'm just thinking about what *could* be."

24

ON HIS WAY back to police headquarters, Deetz called Virgil to make sure the APB for Blaine Milligan was still posted and active. He couldn't believe they hadn't had a sighting yet. Deetz viewed Milligan as a mentally deranged loose cannon who would easily be spotted.

Sunny had warned him otherwise.

Virgil assured him the APB was active.

Deetz's phone buzzed. It was Brandon, the youngest of his two adult boys.

"Hey, son," Deetz answered.

"Dad, hey. Have you heard about Wiley Fleming? He's dead. They assassinated him."

Deetz sighed. *This is not good.*

"I heard he'd been shot, but no . . . I didn't know he died. That's awful."

"Have you seen the video?" Brandon said.

"No."

"Point blank range. There's gonna be a civil war, Dad. People aren't gonna put up with this. I'm not."

Brandon was his conservative, flag-waving, Americana son, while J.P. was the more liberal, justice for all son. Brandon had a gun, J.P. would never think of owning one.

"Just stay away from downtown right now, okay?" Deetz said.

"People have to start standing up to these nuts or we're not going to have a country anymore."

"Brandon, violence in the streets is not going to fix anything; it'll only make it worse. What needs to happen is these people need to be sent home."

"By who, though? The mayor's not doing a thing! She's letting them take over the city," Brandon said.

"I know. I just want *you* to be safe."

"J.P. and Tammy are part of it, you realize that, don't you?"

"I know they're protesting, peacefully."

"How does that make you feel? Protesting to defund the police? What are they thinking?"

"Son, I know these are crazy times, but this will pass."

"They don't want it to pass. They want it to go on like this. They're *forcing* their beliefs on other people. It's not right."

"Just to be clear, you're not calling for any specific reason, like, to tell me anything? Or ask me anything?"

"Have you heard about the Patriots?" Brandon said.

Just what I thought.

"Brandon, do *not* join that group. I can't think of a better, faster way to get yourself arrested—or killed."

Silence.

"Son, I know you have good intentions—"

"Yeah, like protecting our city, protecting cops, protecting innocent people they're harassing. Protecting our heritage."

Deetz couldn't disagree. He wanted the same things.

"Dad, Murph and Luther have been to one of the meetings. The Patriots have a solid plan. They're going to move in and help Portland PD. You should be—"

"That's not how it works, Brandon! They're asking for big trouble if they go in amongst those rioters. People will die."

"How come you let J.P. go in there and not me?"

"I didn't. J.P. is doing that on his own. I told him not to."

"I'm an adult now, too."

"Yes, you are. And I can't stop you from doing anything. But, as someone with thirty-four years of police experience, I can tell you what's going to happen if those Patriots go in there—people will die, possibly *many* people. I love you and that's why I'm asking you not to join up with them and not to go into the city armed and with a grudge."

Deetz sighed. He'd about had it. He was just plain exhausted.

"I carry everywhere I go, just so you know," Brandon said.

The only solace Deetz got from that was that he knew he'd taught Brandon all the ins and outs of gun safety. But Brandon's temperament he couldn't control.

"Just remember, your whole future can be turned upside down if you make one bad move, one bad decision."

"Right, right," Brandon said. "I gotta get rolling."

"Everything's captured on camera these days," Deetz said.

Silence.

"Okay . . . how are classes?" Deetz changed the subject.

"Eh, okay. I'm not crazy about my professors, but what do you expect? This is Portland. Most of them are way out there on the left."

"Grades good?"

"Yeah, yeah."

"How's the internship?" Deetz said.

"Good. I'm pretty much just doing time there, but it's cool."

Deetz had been excited Brandon would get to work at Nike during his senior year and hoped it may even lead to a full-time job.

"Any chance they'll hire you?" Deetz said.

"Eh, maybe. But I'm not sure I'd want to work there."

"Really?" Deetz purposefully sounded shocked.

"Yeah, I mean, the brand is huge and all, but . . . I don't know. The culture . . . We'll see. I've actually been thinking about law enforcement."

Just hit me with a hammer.

In a small way, Deetz was honored Brandon might want to follow in his footsteps, but there were two glaring problems: crime in the U.S. was soaring, and Deetz and Joanie had spent tens of thousands of dollars so Brandon could earn his bachelor's degree and have a professional career.

"Did you hear me?" Brandon said.

"I heard you, but son, you don't need a college degree for that."

"I know. Don't worry, Dad, I'm gonna get my degree." Brandon was agitated. "It's not like I'm gonna quit in the middle of my senior year."

Good. He'll change his mind about being a cop.

"But I'm seriously thinking about it. There's a huge shortage. They're paying like sixty grand a year for entry level."

"Yeah, you know why?" Deetz huffed.

"Of course—"

"Because people are killing cops and because there's so much lawlessness on the streets."

Brandon tried to say something, but Deetz cut him off.

"Because everything cops do is being dissected, analyzed, and scrutinized. We can't even do our jobs anymore without someone second-guessing us—or second-guessing ourselves."

"Somebody's got to serve and protect," Brandon said.

Deetz gave up. "Okay, we'll talk about this. For now, just get your degree, okay?"

Brandon chuckled. "I will, Dad. Don't worry. I'll be off the payroll next Spring."

"I'm not worried about that. We just want you to have your degree. That way you can try what you want and you'll always have that to fall back on."

"Believe me, you and Mom have drilled that into my head," Brandon said.

"Be careful, okay?"

Just as they ended the call, Deetz's phone lit up. "Portland PD ALERT: Officer Wiley Fleming has died from gunshot wounds sustained earlier. The shooter, armed and dangerous, escaped as a passenger in a late model gray Dodge Challenger, Oregon tag 662-FQC. APB has been issued. Car last seen traveling east on SW Salmon St near Multnomah County Courthouse. Description of shooter: white male approximately 25, 6-foot, 160 pounds, long red hair, last seen wearing white hoodie, royal blue sweatpants, white tennis shoes, Dodgers' bandana."

As Deetz entered Portland city limits he slowed and cringed at the toxic smell of smoke and filth, but his blasted window wouldn't go up all the way due to where it had been smashed by that psycho. The buildings and sidewalks were covered in all colors of graffiti with cuss words galore, as well as cop hate and unintelligible gang speak. Glass was shattered all over the streets and the sidewalks were covered thick with trash, broken planters and furniture, bottles, cans, and waste. Deetz could smell urine and feces even with the windows most of the way up.

Brandon should see this . . .

Some store owners and city employees swept up broken glass and scrubbed at graffiti with soapy brushes. Others hammered plywood up in their store windows to keep looters out. A sign in one business window read, "Our windows are shattered, our spirits are shattered."

That about summed it up.

Utterly depressing.

Deetz passed toppled and desecrated statues, blackened cars that had been burned out, and torn down store awnings. One Portland PD cruiser was still ablaze and another, next to it, sat dead at a cockeyed angle with flat tires and a huge concrete blockade smashed through its roof.

A group of about twenty protesters walked and bounced along the sidewalk on the other side of the street, a motley, rag-tag group of all shapes, sizes, and colors—wearing mostly black and donning masks and bandanas to cover their faces; several waved cop hate signs. Luckily, Deetz was not in a patrol car or they might have swarmed him.

He kept a constant eye out for the gray Challenger and for Blaine Milligan's oversized truck, and began to consider what they would do with Sunny that night if Milligan wasn't apprehended by then. Deetz knew there were other shelters in the city for the victims of domestic violence and would ask Callie if she knew of a good one.

His phone buzzed again. This time his caller ID showed it was Stratton & Katz Lumber Company. He answered. It was Sally, the office manager. She sounded elderly, but was completely prepared as she assured Deetz with a quivery voice that Blaine Milligan was a steady employee, on time, good worker, even tied for employee of the month earlier in the year. The address she had for him was in Oatfield, the same one Deetz had struck out on.

Deetz turned into a bank, parked, and jotted down a phone number Sally gave him for Milligan. After they hung up, Deetz compared the number to the one Callie said Milligan had texted her on. It was the same.

Can't hurt to try it.

Deetz dialed the number, not expecting an answer.

Someone picked up, but said nothing.

Deetz's mind scrambled. He hadn't prepared for this.

"Blaine Milligan?" he said.

After a few seconds, a man with a deep voice said, "Wrong number."

Deetz was sure it was Milligan.

"This is Wayne Deetz, Portland PD—"

Click.

The line was dead.

Deetz sat frozen, his heart drumming.

He waited, thought it through, took a deep breath, and called him again—his hands trembling slightly and his temple pounding.

Again, someone at Milligan's end answered but said nothing.

Deetz looked at his notepad and spoke: "Blaine Milligan—Portland PD needs you to turn yourself in. You're being charged with felony domestic violence and assault, credit card theft, breaking and entering, attempted arson, stalking, and other charges." Deetz couldn't believe Milligan hadn't interrupted him. He kept going. "If you turn yourself in, that will be taken into consideration in your court case."

Again, silence.

"Will you turn yourself in?" Deetz said boldly, his heart racing.

He heard Milligan chuckle. "I told you yesterday to stay out of my business. Now you've gone and ruined my truck and got Sunny upset—"

"Turn yourself in, Milligan," Deetz interrupted. "That's the only way this is going to end well."

Milligan lost it and bombarded Deetz with a hot, cantankerous string of expletives.

Deetz repeatedly tried to speak over him and finally did. "If you don't turn yourself in, you will be brought to justice and we'll use every legal means at our disposal to prosecute you to the fullest extent of the law."

"You know what you can do with your court of law, old man?" Milligan blasted Deetz with another vulgar attack.

Deetz tried to speak, but Milligan was yelling now. "You chose the wrong guy to mess with. You think I'm worried about *you* finding *me*?" Milligan laughed. "*You* need to worry about *me*—and what I'm gonna do to Callie Freeland and your sexy little wife."

The line cut dead.

Deetz slammed the phone into the footwell in front of the passenger seat, his blood boiling.

He couldn't take this anymore.

"Why?" he yelled. "Why!"

He ripped his glasses off and covered his face in his hands.

The car was silent, but his ears were ringing like sirens.

He was woozy again.

He draped his arms over the steering wheel and closed his eyes tight.

"Help me . . . Show me what to do."

He tried to still himself.

Focused on breathing.

Cleared his mind.

Then it came to him, very simple and concise: *First thing is Joanie.*

25

Callie drove Tyson's Jeep with Sunny in the passenger seat. They followed Sunny's Focus, driven by Tyson, into a Jacksons gas station and convenience store. Tyson pulled Sunny's car up to a pump and got out to fill it up while Callie parked the Jeep off to the side. Tyson had insisted on driving Sunny's car, just in case Blaine Milligan was following.

"Shoot, I almost forgot, I need to grab a new phone." Sunny opened her door.

"Hold on, I'm coming," Callie said.

They got out and headed for the entrance.

Tyson threw up his hands as if to ask what they were doing.

Callie put a hand up to her ear like a phone.

Tyson nodded, remembering Sunny wanted to get another phone.

Sunny quickly found the rack with the disposable phones and had two in her hands, reading the back of the packages.

Callie stood nearby, scrolling through her phone.

What she wanted to do was get Sunny checked in at Winchester Place and hunker down for the night with Tyson at his house. She'd already arranged to take off of work for the night from the warehouse. She fully expected Deetz and Portland PD to arrest Blaine Milligan soon—if they hadn't already.

Callie looked outside. Tyson had finished filling the tank and was moving the Focus over next to the Jeep.

Sunny had chosen a phone and was paying at the counter.

Callie looked back at her phone and clicked over to Facebook. The red dot at the bottom of the screen told her she had notifications. She tapped.

"Blaine Milligan sent a Facebook message to Callie Freeland."

Callie's insides fused together and her head buzzed with static.

She clicked to read the message:

"Don't close your eyes."

DEETZ WAS ON FULL ALERT, scanning all around as he pulled the Subaru into his neighborhood, then into his driveway and garage. No sign of Blaine Milligan—yet.

As she did so often, Joanie walked out to greet him in the garage, wearing black Yoga pants, a big beige sweater, and moccasins. Her arms were crossed when she got to his door. "Brr. It's freezing out here. What're you doing home?"

Then she noticed the damage to the car and her mouth dropped open as she examined it.

Deetz pointed to the other side of the car, climbed over, and got out the passenger door. "Hi, dear." She came around and stared at him. Her mouth was sealed with a scowl and she shook her head, waiting for an explanation. He kissed her. "I'll tell you all about it. I'm wiped." He got his leather satchel and found his phone on the floor. The screen was cracked from when he'd pitched it.

Idiot.

He briefly explained what happened to the car as they headed inside, making it sound much less dangerous than it had actually been.

"Have you arrested the creep yet? That's all I want to know," Joanie said.

"No. That's what's killing me." Deetz set his stuff on the island in the kitchen, took his coat off and draped it over the back of the chair at Joanie's desk. "He's still out there. Making threats."

"What kind of threats?" Joanie said.

"Hi Daddy." Daughter Leena, 18, came in from the family room. "Catch any bad guys, today?"

Deetz laughed. She said that almost every time he came home. "Hey baby girl. Come here." Deetz hugged her, tight. "No bad guys yet today, but hopefully soon." He eyed Joanie then turned back to Leena. "I thought you worked today?"

"They didn't need me."

"Again?" Deetz said.

She nodded. "Mr. Sanderson said business is way down because of the protesters," Leena said. "I didn't tell him one of my brothers is a protester."

"That's good," Deetz said. "Definitely don't tell Mr. Sanderson that." He and Joanie looked at each other and rolled their eyes.

"Would you tell Mom I don't need to have my wisdom teeth pulled?" Leena said. "She seems in some big hurry and they're not bothering me at all."

"Let me see those wisdom teeth," Deetz said. "Say 'ah.'

Leena opened her mouth. "Ahhhhh."

Deetz looked closely into her mouth. "I don't see them."

Joanie began to protest.

"See, Mom! What's the big fuss about?" Leena said.

"What your father doesn't know yet is that your wisdom teeth are impacted and the longer we wait the worse it will be to get them out," Joanie said, glaring at Deetz.

"Oh, in *that* case," Deetz said, exaggeratedly. "We better do what the dentist says. It'll be fine, honey. They'll give you medicine before so you won't feel anything."

"Brandon said it was a big money-making scheme," Leena said.

Deetz laughed. That sounded like something he would say.

"He also said you can keep your wisdom teeth and it's no big deal," Leena said. "Why would God give you wisdom teeth if he knew they would need to be pulled out? He wouldn't. It makes no sense."

Deetz raised his eyebrows. "She's got a point there."

"Wayne," Joanie said, annoyed. "No, she doesn't. Please. We've discussed this ad nauseum. You're getting your wisdom teeth removed, now let's drop it."

"Anyway, I'm not looking forward to it," Leena said. "I'm gonna have huge squirrel cheeks after. Mom promised me lots and lots of triple chocolate ice cream. As much as I can eat. Right, Mom?

Joanie nodded. "That's right, dear."

Leena looked at Deetz. "Are you down with that?"

Deetz nodded, too. "Oh, absolutely. As much triple choc as you want, for sure."

"Cool." Leena left the kitchen.

Deetz went into the front room and looked out the window for any sign of Blaine Milligan. He heard Joanie come in behind him.

"What's the latest?" she said.

He turned around and put his arms out. "Come here."

They hugged for a long time, then Deetz stepped back and looked at her. "I called him. I never thought he'd answer, but he did. I told him to turn himself in, told him the charges—man, he is one nasty dude."

"What'd he say?"

Deetz didn't want to tell her Milligan had mentioned her name.

"Cussed a blue streak. Just went off. The guy's not right."

"What threats did he make?" Joanie said.

"He said something like, 'You chose the wrong guy to mess with . . . you think I'm worried about you finding me? You should worry about me—what I'm going to do to you.'"

Joanie turned on her heels and headed back into the kitchen.

He was relieved she hadn't pressed him further on specifics, because he knew he couldn't lie to her.

He went back into the kitchen. "It'll be alright, babe. We'll get him."

Joanie put both hands on the island, leaned over, and sighed. "I'm so tired of this."

"I know." Deetz walked over and put a hand on her back.

"It's not enough that I have to worry about you every day, whether you'll come home or not, whether you'll be shot or end up in the hospital." Joanie stood, crossed her arms and faced him. "This is personal, Wayne. Personal! Our home. Our family. Not enough money in the world could make this worth it."

A tear streaked down her cheek.

Deetz stepped closer and wiped it away. "Don't cry."

Joanie pushed his hand away. "Just quit. Quit! Forget the darn retirement package. What's that going to be worth if you're in a wheelchair—or dead?"

"Honey, once we get this guy it's over."

"You know how often you say things like that? 'Once this happens, it'll be over? Once that happens, it'll be over.' But it's never over. Look at our lives the past three years."

"Well, we're in this thing now with this guy, so quitting wouldn't make any difference—"

"Blah, blah, blah." Joanie threw open the dishwasher and began putting the clean dishes away, with an attitude.

Deetz went over and pulled the silverware basket from the dishwasher. He set it on the counter and quietly began putting the silverware away.

Deetz stopped what he was doing and faced Joanie. "Do you really want me to quit?"

She took a deep breath and sighed aloud. "I've been praying that I could stop worrying about you. But the last few years, my gosh, Wayne . . . the shootings, Leena's kidnapping, now this."

"I know. I'm so tired, babe. I know what you're saying. I'm with you. We've got a decision to make."

Joanie stepped closer to him and looked up into his eyes. He took her in his arms and leaned back against the island counter. He held her close. She squeezed him and said, "Pray for us."

Deetz paused, then spoke quietly: "God, protect us tonight. Protect Sunny and Callie and Tyson. Bring this guy to justice. Put him away for a long time. Help Sunny start over . . . And please, show us what to do about my job. You know we're struggling. Help us know what you want. Help us make a decision and stick with it, knowing we can rest in your plan."

They both whispered, "Amen," and held each other there.

26

———

Sunny was in her bedroom, packing a big suitcase with clothes, shoes, and other stuff she hadn't had time or space to pack the night before. Her whole body ached and she had a splitting headache. She hopped out to the kitchen to get her bottle of vitamins to pack. She and Callie and Tyson had managed to get her car safely back into the garage with a full tank of gas.

Callie was emptying the vacuum in the garage. Tyson was in the front room talking to Detective Deetz on the phone. She'd overheard Tyson tell Deetz about the cryptic Facebook message Blaine had sent Callie, that read: "Don't close your eyes."

In order to listen in on Tyson's conversation, Sunny sprayed down the kitchen counter and began cleaning it with paper towels.

"You're saying you actually talked to him? And he threatened Joanie and Callie?" Tyson spoke into the phone, then listened for Deetz's response.

"So, what do we do?" Tyson said.

He listened.

"Okay. Once we get her checked in, what do you think Callie and I should do?" Tyson said. "Stay at my place again?"

Sunny knew they were planning to take her to a shelter, the one Blaine didn't know about. Part of her wanted to go along with it. Wait for Blaine's arrest. Get back to living her life, in her house, with her job.

But that would mean testifying in court and all the publicity and nonsense that would surely come with it. Plus, she'd had such bad luck her entire life, she didn't think Blaine would be caught. Even if he was, she didn't believe they would be able to keep him locked up. *Never.* He was uncanny in that way. Ever since she knew him, he was like Houdini, working his way out of any predicament. He'd once gotten taken in for questioning in a robbery case and came to her place two hours later, laughing about it, bragging that he had nine lives.

Sunny had never forgotten that.

Neither had she forgotten his vehement vow to never, ever return to prison.

She tried to reassure herself that he was brought to justice once and served time. *It can happen again. It has to happen again.*

"So, you're working from home?" Tyson continued speaking to Deetz on the phone.

"You guys can stay at my place if you want," Tyson said. "It'd be cramped, but we could make it work."

Sunny couldn't shake the guilt of getting Callie involved with Blaine, which led to Deetz being involved, and Tyson. Even if she left town safely right that minute, their lives would still be in peril. Part of her felt she owed it to them to do as they said, go to the shelter, wait for Blaine's arrest.

Tyson came into the kitchen. He was off the phone.

Callie walked into the house with the vacuum cleaner. "What'd Deetz say?"

"He got through to Milligan on the phone," Tyson said. "Told him to turn himself in."

"I'm sure that went over well," Sunny said.

Tyson chuckled. "Yeah. He proceeded to threaten . . . basically all of us."

"What did he say, exactly?" said Callie, staring at Tyson—who hesitated.

"He mentioned Joanie and Sunny . . . and you," Tyson said.

Sunny looked at Callie. Their eyes locked. Callie shook her head and rolled the vacuum into the kitchen. "I'm not worried about it," she said. "They'll get him."

Sunny had no words.

This is my fault.

"You ready for me to check your foot again?" Callie said.

That does it.

"Why are you being so nice to me?" Sunny said. "Why are you even still here? I've done nothing but mess up your lives." She began to cry.

Callie went over, put an arm around Sunny, and led her hobbling over to the couch. "Come on, sit."

They plopped down on the couch next to each other.

"You're my friend," Callie said. "Friends help each other."

"If I was you, I would have bailed on this friendship a long time ago," Sunny said.

Callie slipped down to her knees. "Let's see your foot."

Sunny lifted her left leg and rested her foot on the coffee table.

Gently, Callie removed the white tape, lifted the gauze from the top of Sunny's foot, and examined it closely. Sunny didn't want to look at it, didn't care.

"It's looking fairly good," Callie said. "How does it feel?"

Sunny shrugged. "About the same."

"I don't think we need to do anything to it right now." Callie replaced the gauze and refastened the tape. "You remember I told you I was in a toxic relationship once?"

Sunny nodded.

"The last time," Callie said, "he broke my nose and cracked four ribs."

Sunny cussed.

Callie sat back down on the couch next to Sunny. "He apologized all over himself. Cried. It was pitiful. Thank God, something in me told me to get out that time. That's when I found the Dorcas House. The counselors were a godsend. I quit my job, stayed away from my folks and brothers, just healed there."

"What happened to him?" Sunny said.

"A friend told me later he was going berserk trying to track me down. She said he threatened to kill me—and himself. I know he would have done it the next time I saw him. But there wasn't a next time."

"What'd he do?" Sunny said.

"He was one of the first ones killed in the mass shooting on Pioneer Square."

Sunny sat there, stunned. Finally, she whispered, "No way."

Callie nodded. "Yep."

"That's cuz you love God. He did that. He protected you," Sunny said.

Callie chuckled. "Well, what's interesting is, about a month before he broke my nose, that's when I found my little church. I'd been going for four weeks. It was all new to me. It breathed new life into me. And then Keith beat me that next time, that last time, and something finally clicked inside me. I *knew* it was time to go and I'd never had the strength or resolve to leave before."

"So, God got you out, then brought the hammer down on old Keithy Boy."

Callie chuckled again.

"You're a good person," Sunny said.

"No, actually I'm not. I'm a sinner, just like everyone else," Callie said. "I just realized I couldn't live life in my own strength, so I surrendered everything to Christ. Everything."

"What does that even mean?" Sunny said.

The window shattered.

Callie screamed.

Fire danced across the floor and ran up the curtains.

Cold air blew in, fanning the flames.

Sunny knew instantly, Blaine had thrown a Molotov Cocktail. She stood but figured Callie would be faster. "Grab the fire extinguisher," Sunny yelled, "under the kitchen sink!"

Callie ran, dodging glass shards.

"I'll be right there," Tyson yelled from the doorway.

Sunny grabbed a cushion from the couch, hopped over and began smacking it against the flames on the floor.

The smell of fuel overpowered her.

Tyson ran in, ripped the blanket off the bed, and repeatedly whacked at the flames creeping up the wall.

Callie showed up with the extinguisher. Tyson threw the blanket down, grabbed it, fiddled with the pin forever, and finally sprayed that sucker everywhere.

Sunny hopped as fast as she could to the other window and peered out back.

No sign of Blaine.

"I'm going for the cops." Tyson handed the extinguisher to Callie. "Maybe we can still catch him."

Sunny knew they wouldn't.

He has nine lives.

27

─────────

Deetz worked away at the desk in his study, sipping hot cocoa Joanie had just delivered. The beautiful afternoon had turned dark and the wind howled outside, making the window rattle at times. He'd received the video footage he'd been waiting for—showing Milligan raising havoc outside Callie's warehouse, and dousing the hallway outside her apartment with gas. He'd just hung up with his boss, Sergeant Tidwell, after explaining background and details about the manhunt for Blaine Milligan and telling him why he was working from home—because Joanie had been threatened.

Tidwell had told him Portland PD was gearing up for a night of serious violence, especially in the aftermath of officer Wiley Fleming's murder that afternoon. Tidwell was calling in virtually every officer who could work, because they were expecting emotional clashes between anti-police protestors and those who may come out in support of the police and to condemn the execution-style assassination of Wiley Fleming.

Tidwell said a huge group of Portland Patriots showed up at Wiley Fleming's house, offering their support. Wiley's brother, Denver Fleming, stood outside the small west end bungalow, telling a mob of reporters that he and his family were horrified and outraged at the murder of his brother, and were prepared to "fight back" against anti-police protestors.

So, a nasty storm was brewing on several fronts, and Deetz prayed his sons had the sense to stay clear of trouble. In fact, he got out his phone to shoot them a quick text—and it rang. It was Callie Freeland.

"We were sitting in Sunny's house and a Molotov Cocktail crashed through the window," she said, her voice trembling. "We got the fire out before it did a lot of damage."

Deetz shot to his feet and crossed to the window. "Did they nail him?"

"No. This was at the back of the house. The police never saw anything. Tyson just talked to them," Callie said.

"Was anyone hurt?"

"No. But Wayne, I'm worried."

"I know, I know," Deetz said. "Do I need to come over?"

His mind spun. He didn't want to leave Joanie and Leena.

"I don't think so. Tyson's got to cover up the broken window. I think he's going to nail a tarp up there for now."

Deetz squeezed the back of his neck and sighed. He was flabbergasted.

"The police are parking right in Sunny's driveway from now on," Callie said. "One will sit in the car there and the other will sit out back, or even just inside the back door."

"This guy's so brazen. I'm starting to think Sunny's right—he's on a suicide mission. Where's Sunny's car?"

"We got it. Filled the tank. It's here in the garage."

"You know the shelters in the city, what's another good one?"

"Winchester Place. Patrick Avenue," Callie said. "Sunny just had an idea. She got a new phone when we got gas, so she's ready to pitch the old one. What if we turn on location services on the old phone, give it to a cop who's driving her car, and have the cop drive around until Milligan comes looking for her?"

Deetz paced. It wasn't a bad idea. The problem was, it would require him to cut through all kinds of red tape to get it approved, especially if they planned to use Sunny's car; it would be a legal nightmare.

"Wayne?"

"I'm thinking," he said.

He could hear Sunny and Tyson talking in the background.

"Let me think about it some more," Deetz said. "I might make some calls to see if it's feasible."

"It's getting late," Callie said. "We can either stay here at Sunny's with the police or check her in at Winchester Place."

"Then what? What would you and Tyson do?"

"Stay at his place, I guess," Callie said. "Unless you have a better idea."

"There's no way those officers wouldn't have seen his truck," Deetz said. "I'm thinking he's in a different vehicle."

Silence.

"This is creeping me out," Callie finally said.

"I know," Deetz said. "I'm trying to figure out his motives. What does he want? Does he just want Sunny? Or . . ."

Deetz stopped, realizing he was about to freak Callie out even more by insinuating Milligan wanted to take them all down.

"I think we need to take her to the shelter," Callie whispered. "This is exactly what it's for. She'll be safe there and they can help get the healing process started."

Deetz wrestled with it, but knew they had to do something. It was almost dark. "Okay," he said, "but I'll take her."

He had to be absolutely sure Sunny wasn't followed. Plus, an idea was formulating in the back of his mind that had to do with Sunny's phone.

"Do me a favor," Deetz said. "Have Sunny packed and ready to go. Have her old phone charged. But give me an hour or two. I've got some research to do and some other stuff." He had to make sure Joanie and Leena were safe.

"Okay," Callie said. "So, we'll see you here in about an hour?"

"Yeah. I'll call you if it changes. I've got to think it through. But yes, if you don't hear from me, I'll be there in an hour—give or take."

They hung up.

Deetz went back to the window, which was now being pelted with rain. He finished off the cocoa, thinking perhaps the bad weather would deter Milligan, and the mob downtown.

"You want spaghetti noodles or tube noodles?" came Leena's voice from the doorway.

Deetz turned around. "I don't care, honey."

"Would you say spaghetti? I hate the tube noodles."

He laughed and took the empty cup over to her. "Oh, for sure, spaghetti then."

Leena took the cup from him. "Good call." Then she left.

Deetz turned back to the window. He could just barely see the tops of the tall blowing trees through the reflection from his office lights.

He thought through the various options. He could have Joanie and Leena go to Joanie's sister's place in Beaverton. Then he could get Sunny's phone, turn on location services, and wait for Milligan to show up at the house.

Or, he could station a cop outside the house to watch over Joanie and Leena, and he could take Sunny's phone someplace else to draw Milligan out.

But there was no guarantee Milligan would take the bait, in fact, he probably wouldn't. He was as streetwise as they came.

Deetz went back to his desk and sat down. He ripped a sheet of paper from a pad on which he'd written the names and addresses of two women Milligan had victimized in the past who still lived in the Portland area. One was a trespassing and strangulation victim, the other was an assault victim who'd been harassed and menaced by Milligan. Also on the paper was the name and address of Milligan's sister, Bridget Reedy, who lived just outside Portland.

Next, he called Virgil at Portland PD headquarters and explained he wanted three different officers to go to the residences of Milligan's sister and his two past victims.

"Wayne, I can't do it," Virgil said. "We need everybody we have in the streets tonight. This thing's gonna be chaos. You've heard, right?"

"Yeah," Deetz hesitated. He was in such a hard place. If Milligan hadn't threatened Joanie, he could be out making these calls himself. Instead, he was stuck there.

"Wayne, I gotta go, man," Virgil said.

"Can you spare one officer?" Deetz said. "Joanie and Leena are here, and I need to leave to get Sunny to the shelter."

"You already have two at Sunny's house," Virgil said. "You're killing me here."

"Virgil, any other time this would be a no brainer. Come on, man. My family's in danger."

There was a long pause.

"I'll see what I can do, Wayne. I'll be in touch." Virgil hung up.

Deetz knew if it was at all feasible, Virgil would come through.

But he couldn't count on it.

He sat there with his elbows on his desk, thinking. Thinking about everything. About where Blaine Milligan was at that moment, and what he was planning. About keeping Joanie and Leena out of harm's way. About his sons. Where were they? Hoping they had the sense not to be downtown amidst the rioting. About getting Sunny to the shelter without being followed. About Callie and Tyson staying overnight at his place, worrying about Blaine Milligan showing up all night long.

And, he thought about quitting.

Being done with the stress of this job.

Going to bed in peace. Waking in peace.

But that would have to wait.

He got up, went to the closet, got his holster and gun, and strapped them on. As he checked his magazine and dropped a spare in his back pocket, he had an idea. He got out his phone and called Brandon.

Amazingly, he answered. "What's up?"

"Hey son, you busy?" Deetz said.

"Why? What's going on?"

Deetz walked to the door and closed it gently. "It's a long story, but there's a fugitive on the loose. He's terrorizing a local woman. You know Callie and Tyson—they're trying to help this lady, and so am I. But this guy, this fugitive, has threatened all of us."

"Sheesh, Dad."

"There's an APB out for him. I've got to go help this lady get to a shelter, but I can't leave the house."

"Why not?"

"He threatened me . . . and your mom," Deetz said quietly.

"Mom? What the heck?" Brandon said.

"Bottom line, I'm wondering if you can arm up and come over? Maybe even stay the night?"

"Hmm . . ."

"You have plans?" Deetz was thinking he may be killing two birds with one stone by keeping Brandon away from the riots and hiring him as a bodyguard.

"I'll come," Brandon said. "My first class isn't till eleven tomorrow so I should be okay. You need me to stay over?"

"Not sure yet, but it's great you can if we need you. Thanks, son."

"When do you need me?" Brandon said.

"Like, right now."

28

CALLIE TURNED on the floodlights and stood shivering in the small backyard at Sunny's house, wishing she'd worn more than a hoodie. It was dark, drizzling, and windy; a big storm was brewing. She watched as Tyson and one of the two Portland PD officers, Tom Hood, a hulking young guy, fought the wind while trying to hammer a royal blue plastic tarp up over the smashed window.

Deetz would be arriving within an hour to take Sunny to Winchester Place, the domestic violence shelter over on Patrick Avenue. Sunny was inside getting the house the way she wanted before what could be an extended leave.

Callie hoped and prayed everything would go smoothly getting Sunny settled, keeping her and Tyson and Deetz's family safe, and apprehending Blaine Milligan. She examined the blackened wood around the smashed window and still couldn't believe Milligan had the audacity to firebomb Sunny's house—with them inside.

The wind whipped the wet tarp, which Sunny had borrowed from a neighbor next door. Tyson and Tom laughed as they worked together to flatten it and get it secured. Tyson was up on a ladder, hammering away. Tom was standing on the ground handing Tyson nails and making sure the tarp was even and tight. They were talking like long lost friends. The other cop, Rocky somebody, was sitting in the Portland PD patrol car, which was backed into Sunny's driveway around the front of the house. They were making

144

it obvious now they were there to protect the place. Callie wondered why they hadn't done that in the first place? Probably because they never thought anyone would be brazen enough to sabotage the place with a police car and two officers sitting directly across the street.

The rain came harder. "I'm going in, guys," she called as she opened the door. "Need anything?"

"We're good," Tyson said. "Hey Freeland . . ."

Callie stopped and looked at Tyson.

"Tom thinks it may be safer for us to stay here tonight," Tyson said. "They'll be here all night. Safer than us staying at my place. What do you think? Maybe we should ask Sunny if it's okay with her?"

Callie shrugged. "I guess that's a good idea. I'll talk to Sunny." She ducked inside and Sunny was standing right there.

"That is a good idea," Sunny said, as Callie shut the glass door closed and relished the warmth of the house. "Definitely stay here, where you have police protection."

Callie did like the idea. "You sure?" she said.

Sunny nodded. "Absolutely. You guys can stay here as long as you want. By the way, I got a hold of a handyman, Kurt or Kirk. He'll be here to fix the window late morning tomorrow. If you're here, great. But no one has to be here. I made arrangements with him to fix it and lock up when he's done."

Sunny walked into the kitchen. "I made a big pot of coffee. You need to have dinner. There's pasta and spaghetti sauce in the pantry and frozen pizzas in the freezer," she said. "Help yourself to anything that looks good."

"What about you?" Callie said.

"I had a peanut butter and jelly sandwich. I'm good."

"Are you nervous? How're you feeling?"

Sunny stared at Callie. "I'm worried about you guys and about Deetz and his wife." She shook her head and looked down. "He's a lunatic. He won't stop—until someone stops him. He won't. So, I'm afraid, even if I'm safely hidden, he'll pick the next best thing— you guys."

That gave Callie the creeps.

The hammering was loud. She walked across the kitchen until

she was four feet from Sunny. "It's going to be okay, Sunny," Callie nodded, reassuringly. "Really. It's going to be fine. I trust that."

"What'd you mean earlier about surrendering?" Sunny said. "You didn't finish."

Callie got chills. She chuckled and felt a spark of hope inside.

"Back when Keith was abusing me and I found my little church, that's where I ended up realizing I needed God in my life. I gave up trying to live in my own strength," Callie said. "It was like I just collapsed at God's feet and said, 'Here, take my soul, take my life. I've made a mess of it.' I surrendered. And now, I try to let him, his Spirit, live through me. I try to hear his voice and let him guide me. I rely on him, not me."

"Dang, girl, that is deep," Sunny said. "But you make it sound *so real*. And I know it's not just talk. I've always known there was something different about you, ever since the first time we saw each other at aerobics. You have this peace about you. You're always so positive and upbeat."

"Aw, that's nice of you to say. Maybe when this all blows over, you can come to church with me."

Sunny bit her bottom lip and looked at Callie, her eyes glistening.

"What's wrong?"

Sunny shook her head concisely and looked away, a tear streaking down her pretty face.

Callie stepped closer. "What is it?"

Without looking at Callie, Sunny said softly, "I never had a friend like you. No one stays with me very long."

Callie reached out and Sunny embraced her. They hugged and Sunny cried.

"I'll always be your friend," Callie said.

"You're a good person," Sunny said. "I'd like to be more like you."

Callie leaned back and smiled at her and a tear shot down her own face. "We're the same, my friend. Life's tough . . . It's so hard. Everybody has trouble. We'll get through it, together, okay?"

Sunny buried her head in Callie's shoulder, nodded, and hugged her tightly. "Thank you," Sunny said. "I never would've survived without you."

A knock at the front door startled them both.

They looked at each other.

"I'll have Tom go." Callie hurried to the back door and told the officer someone was knocking at the front door. He and Tyson, both soaked, were bringing in the ladder and tools, and had been standing there jabbering.

Officer Tom wiped his feet on a rug inside the door and headed for the front door with his right hand on his holstered weapon.

The knock came again, softly.

Tom looked through the peep hole. "Oh, sheesh, it's just Rocky." He unbolted the door. "Bet he needs to use the facilities; he has to go more than any partner I've ever had."

Callie, Sunny, and Tyson chuckled and let out a cumulative sigh of relief.

Tom pulled the door open and began to kid Rocky about his weak bladder.

But Tom jumped back in shock and frantically went for his gun.

A gun blast from just outside the door spun Tom and he dropped to the ground. His gun clattered to the floor five feet from him. Wincing and grabbing his bleeding left shoulder, Tom yelled, "Run! Get out!"

Callie and Sunny grabbed each other, turned and ran for the back door, ducking as they went.

Tyson bent to one knee and ripped up the cuff of his pants in a frantic effort to get the gun from his ankle holster.

Blaine Milligan burst into the room clutching Rocky in a choke-hold and pointing a large black gun sideways like a hoodlum. In one sweeping blur he wrenched Rocky's neck and let him crumple to the ground unconscious, kicked Tom's gun away, and blasted Tyson from twenty feet away.

Callie screamed as blood spurted from Tyson's leg. He cried out in pain and toppled over to the floor, gushing blood from his right thigh.

"Get my gun!" Tyson screamed at Callie.

"Sunny, get out!" Callie pushed Sunny toward the back door, then dashed to the floor next to Tyson, crying and fumbling frantically for his gun.

"Don't." Milligan was upon them in several large strides. He squeezed Callie's shoulder like a vice and shoved her sprawling to the floor. She screamed.

"Leave her alone!" Tyson yelled.

Milligan backhanded him in the face, drawing blood instantly from his mouth.

"Unbuckle the holster and give it to me," Milligan ordered Callie and surveyed the room, settling his eyes on Sunny, who was cowering at the back door.

Callie's ears rang from the gunshots.

She could smell the gun powder in the air.

Her heart pounded.

She was nauseous with fear.

This has to be a bad dream.

Sunny was frozen on her knees at the back door, her hands in the air, looking out into the night, knowing what was coming.

29

———————

Deetz was on the phone in his study, attempting to reach Blaine Milligan's two past victims, who still lived in the area, as well as Milligan's sister. Son Brandon had arrived looking like he was on some kind of undercover assault team. He lugged a large, black leather satchel in which he carried two impressive, expensive, powerful handguns, multiple magazines, and several boxes of ammo for each.

It actually pleased Deetz that Brandon had taken an interest in firearms. After the Pioneer Square shootings, then the foiled copycat attempt a year later, Brandon had asked Deetz to teach him to "shoot." They'd spent a lot of enjoyable father-son time at the shooting range and Deetz had complete confidence in Brandon's ability to handle guns safely. Brandon was, in fact, an excellent marksman.

Since Deetz was going to be leaving soon to get Sunny to the shelter, he wanted Joanie to have a gun at her bedside that night. He had once taught her how to handle and fire a gun at the range, but it had been years ago, so Brandon was giving her a quick refresher course in the kitchen while eating a huge bowl of spaghetti.

Neither of Blaine Milligan's past two local victims—Angie Valdez or Brenda Marks—answered Deetz's calls, so he left messages with both, saying it was a courtesy call from Portland PD, checking in to see how they were doing.

Deetz dialed the last number on his list, Milligan's sister, Bridget Reedy.

Right then, Leena showed up in his doorway again. "Dad, if Brandon and Mom have guns, I need one, too."

Bridget Reedy's phone continued to ring.

"No honey. You have to know all about gun safety before using a gun," Deetz said.

"What am I supposed to do if this nutter shows up?" Leena said.

The woman Deetz was calling answered, "Hello."

Deetz waved Leena out and motioned for her to shut the door.

"Hello . . . is this Bridget Reedy?" Deetz said.

"Who's calling?"

"Detective Wayne Deetz, Portland Police."

"Oh, here we go."

"I'm calling about Blaine Milligan."

Silence.

"Is he indeed your brother, Miss Reedy?" Deetz said.

"Ha. I can't lie to the police, can I?"

"No. Best not to."

"He is," she said.

"Have you seen him lately?" Deetz said.

Again, silence.

"He's wanted right now on some extremely serious charges," Deetz said. "People's lives are in danger. Please tell me the truth."

"He needs help," she said. "He's not right in the head. Seriously. Are you aware of that?"

"Have you seen him recently?" Deetz insisted.

"He's bipolar. Possibly schizophrenic—"

"We understand that. Have you seen him?"

"It was late last night. Real late."

After he followed Sunny to the Dorcas House.

"What happened?" Deetz said.

"Knock at the back door. Scared the heck out of us. My boyfriend went. It was Blaine. He barged in. Said he needed a place to sleep for a few hours. Didn't give us any choice."

"What time was that?"

"One-thirty maybe?"

Deetz jotted it down. "Did he say anything about where he'd been or what he was doing?"

"Are you kidding me? We barely talk. We put him in the spare bedroom. He was gone by the time we got up in the morning."

"What time was that?"

"Eight, eight-thirty."

Late sleepers.

"What time did he leave, exactly?"

"Sometime between one-thirty and eight. We didn't hear him go. Hold on . . . Did you hear him go?" She was yelling to someone else, the boyfriend, probably. "Neither of us heard him leave. He probably only stayed a few hours. He doesn't sleep. That's one of his problems. He's like, nocturnal. When he got into his teenage years, he would sit in a chair all night and just stare out the window."

"Did he leave anything with you? Does he keep any of his things at your place?"

"No."

"You live where, exactly?" Deetz said.

"Crestview. Northeast of the city, toward the airport."

"Do you know Sunny?"

"No."

"The woman he lives with sometimes?"

"I know he shacks up with someone. But that's what he does. Goes from one to another. We don't talk, okay? It's a very strained relationship, if you can even call it that."

"Did he say he might be back?" Deetz asked.

"Look, my boyfriend opened the door to the spare room and that was it. Nothing was said, other than he needed a place."

"Has he stayed with you like this any other time, recently?"

"Hadn't seen him in months."

"You can see my number, right?" Deetz said.

"Uh huh."

"If he shows up, any time day or night, I need you to call this number. You'll get me, personally. Try to stall him until I get there." He asked for her exact address, which he wrote down.

"What's he done?" she said.

"Felony domestic violence, arson, harassment, among other things. So, if he does show up, you're under obligation to let me know. If you don't, you can be charged with aiding and abetting."

Deetz wrapped up the call and joined Brandon, Joanie, and Leena in the kitchen.

"Virgil called the house line because he couldn't get you on your cell," Joanie said. "He freed up a unit for tonight, for here."

"Thank God," Deetz said. "Good man."

"Any more word on this creep's whereabouts or anything?" Joanie said.

Deetz could tell she was frustrated, and apprehensive about the night ahead.

"Talked to his sister," Deetz said. "He crashed at her place in Crestview late last night. We'll get him."

Joanie rolled her eyes, finished packing a small brown paper bag, and slid it over to him. "Snack for later."

Deetz went over and kissed her forehead. "Thank you, dear. Brandon get you all up to snuff?" He nodded toward the guns on the counter.

She raised her eyebrows and nodded, with her mouth sealed. What that meant was, yes, she was 'up to snuff,' but, no, she did not want to be put in the position of having him leave the house with a maniac on the loose.

Brandon was in the family room helping Leena find something on TV.

Deetz drew Joanie close and put his arms around her. She rested her head against his chest and hugged him. They stood like that, embracing each other in silence.

She'd been so good—so patient.

He looked at the long paper chain draped over the refrigerator. He'd tear off another ring the next morning and they'd keep going.

"Maybe we should move," Joanie said, with her head still resting on his chest.

"Wow. Where'd that come from?"

"I don't think the city's ever going to be the same," she said.

They'd talked about downsizing when Brandon finished college, but they'd never discussed moving away from Portland.

"Where?" he said.

"I was reading about best places to retire." She leaned back and looked up at him. "The Southeast has a great climate. Close to mountains *and* beaches."

"Southeast as in Charlotte? Atlanta?"

"Charlotte, maybe. Atlanta's too big. But Asheville's supposed to be really cool, kind of like the Portland of the east—without the crime."

"Hmm. We can look at it, online."

"I was thinking maybe we could get an Airbnb, just explore. You've got vacation time that you need to take, Mister."

It actually sounded good. Really good.

"Let's set some time aside, look at the calendar, check out some places," he said. "I'd like that."

She hugged him.

He did the same.

"We're a good team," he said.

"Be careful."

"I will."

He wanted to say the same to her, but didn't want to scare her.

"Yo Dad, backup's here," Brandon called from the front foyer. "One of the new Crown Vic's. Check it out. He's got those low-key blue light bars."

Deetz kissed Joanie, squeezed her hands, and went to the front door.

"You think he'll keep those lights on all night?" Brandon stood with the front door wide open as the wind and rain whipped outside.

Deetz got to him and they stepped onto the small porch and shut the door. The Portland PD black and white was parked at the curb at the end of the driveway, about eighty feet away, directly in front of the house. As Brandon said, three low-key blue light bars glowed in the storm.

"You gonna talk to him?" Brandon said.

"On my way out," Deetz said. "It's freezing. Come on." Deetz led the way back inside and squared up with Brandon, who was about as tall as him now.

"You've seen what this guy looks like, right?" Deetz said.

Brandon nodded. "I've stalked him online."

"You'll be fine. Keep your ears open. Protect your Mom and sister at all costs."

Brandon nodded. "You be careful."

Deetz went to the closet, threw on his parka, and made sure he had the address for Winchester Place. Out of Joanie's sight, he double-checked his gun—magazine full, spare magazine in pocket.

From what he'd seen and learned of Blaine Milligan, if the guy wanted to do harm, a lone squad car sitting in front of a house wasn't going to stop him.

Deetz needed to go get him.

And that's what he intended to do.

30

———

In that terrifying moment, trembling in fear at the back door of her house with wind and rain pelting the tarp that covered the window, Sunny simply went numb.

Blaine's gunshots blared in her ears and she seemed to be floating above herself, in shock.

His presence, his control—was palpable.

Their only hope was Wayne Deetz, who was supposedly on his way.

But Sunny had the dreadful, sick feeling Deetz would die that night. They all would.

And it'll be my fault.

In silence, Blaine marched through the small house, snatching Tom's gun from the floor, locking the doors, hand-cuffing the two officers together and taking the keys, emptying Tyson's gun, and now, peering out the front window. As always, he was in absolute control.

Callie had ripped off her hoodie and was pressing hard against the gunshot wound that had opened up Tyson's thigh. She was panicked and sweating, even though the cold wind was seeping in around the broken window just feet away. Tyson and Callie were whispering. Little did they know, nothing they planned could stop whatever Blaine was about to do.

The one officer who'd been shot, Tom, had sat up on the floor and was leaning against the wall, clutching his left shoulder, trying to stop the bleeding, and trying to revive Rocky at the same time.

Surely Deetz will see the empty police car out front.

Blaine marched in like Rambo. "All phones, radios out here." He knelt and patted Rocky down until he found his phone, then ripped his radio off his belt. "Hurry up," he said to Tom, who was fumbling for his phone and radio with his one bloody, free hand. Blaine took their electronics to the kitchen and threw them in the sink. He turned the water on, then the disposal, and began shoving the phones and radios down the hole.

With the disturbing, crushing, clattering noise of the disposal, Blaine was giving the others a taste of what Sunny already knew— he was a raging psycho bent on shock, terror, and control. And if his life ended that night, it would be fine with him.

Finally, he turned off the water and disposal and sauntered over to Callie and Tyson, motioning for them to hand over their phones. "Turn 'em on. Get 'em open so I can see." When they did, he grabbed them, straightened up, and eyed Sunny.

She almost lost control of her bladder.

A high-pitched siren of terror blared in her head and her stomach churned with bile.

He stepped over to her with his big hand out. "Phone. On and open."

She had both phones with her. She'd already decided she was going to give him the old one, the one he knew about. She would keep the new one, thinking she might be able to call for help at some point. She knew she was taking a gamble, but figured she was going to die anyway, so why not die trying to fight?

"This should be good," Blaine said, as he snatched the phone from Sunny's trembling hand, crossed to a couch, plunked down with a sigh, and dropped all the phones clacking onto the coffee table. "We'll start with Tyson's."

"My partner needs to be revived or he's gonna die," Tom said from his position on the floor beyond Blaine.

Blaine glared over at the two cops, both of them a bloody mess from Tom's gunshot wound and from Tom trying to revive Rocky. Blaine said nothing for a moment, as if he held Rocky's life in his hands and was about to decide whether he would live or die. With his eyes still on them he said, "Sunny, get a bowl of ice water and throw it on the pig's face."

The orders began.

Sunny grunted as she stood. Dizzy, she clutched the back of a chair to steady herself. It all felt like an eerie dream. Although she'd managed to get a loose-fitting shoe on her injured foot, blood had seeped through. She watched Blaine scrolling through Tyson's phone as she limped to the kitchen.

"So, you've been talking to Wayne Deetz," Blaine said, loudly. "Most recent, just this afternoon. No big surprise." He clicked his tongue several times and scrolled more. "Oh, listen to this . . . a text from Wayne Deetz, calling me a 'wingnut!'"

Not good.

"Tyson needs to get to a hospital," Callie said, frantically, as she continued to press the blood-soaked hoodie against his wound. "Please, he's losing too much blood."

Blaine laughed, tossed Tyson's phone onto the table, and picked up Callie's. "Let's see what you've been up to, Miss Callie." He looked over at her. "You didn't accept my Friend request yet." He chuckled. "You and me are gonna have some fun, later. A little something for you to look forward to."

Tyson fumed. He was sweating and pale. His eyes searched the room, the other faces, seeking some way to overcome Milligan; probably hoping Deetz would somehow save the day.

Sunny got a plastic bowl from the cupboard and went to fill it with cold water. Small pieces of phones and radios littered the sink.

This is Blaine's usual motive. He's already decided he's going to do something diabolical, but he'll have fun with it, build up to it, enjoy the terror he'll create along the way.

"Oops, yours turned off." Blaine stood and took Callie's phone to her. "Get me back in there." He handed it to her and looked down at Tyson. "Man, you *have* lost a lot of blood." He walked to the closest window, yanked a thin curtain from its rod, went back and tossed it to Callie. She handed him the phone, discarded the bloody hoodie, and pressed the curtain against the wound; Tyson winced and shook his head. "Why are you doing this?" he said. "We haven't done anything to you. Just let us go. At least let the girls go."

No. Don't say that . . .

Blaine's face went sour. He clenched his jaw and booted Tyson as hard as he could in the side of his rib cage.

Callie screamed and lurched at Blaine, who roared with laughter.

Tyson grimaced loudly and buried his head in his arms.

Blaine stood over Tyson and Callie, scrolling through her phone.

Sunny started to take the bowl of water to Tom and Rocky, hoping it would distract Blaine from Callie's phone. Leaving the kitchen, she noticed the full pot of hot coffee she'd made earlier and stopped. It would turn off by itself soon. To keep it from doing so, she made sure Blaine wasn't looking and quickly turned the machine off and on so the coffee would remain hot two more hours.

She had to find a way to fight back, to stop him.

She just hoped Deetz would notice something off and call for backup.

She made her way to Rocky and Tom, sloshing the bowl of water as she limped.

"You talked to that cop one hour ago?" Blaine yelled at Callie. "What's going on?" He grabbed Callie by the hair and yanked her head back. Tyson lunged for him but buckled over in pain. Blaine shoved Callie's head away and stomped Tyson hard in the stomach, knocking the wind out of him. "What's going on?" Blaine demanded. "Is that pig coming here?"

That's when Blaine looked up and locked eyes with Sunny.

He marched directly at her, snatched the bowl of water, threw it on Rocky's face, and slammed the bowl clattering to the floor. Rocky shook and choked and coughed. Tom leaned over, in obvious pain himself, and patted him hard on the back. "Rocky, man, you hear me? Breathe, bro. Breathe."

Blaine stopped and focused again on Callie's phone, tapping and scrolling. Sunny squirmed. *Not good. Not good . . .*

"Okay, Deetz took photos of the gas at Callie's . . . getting video footage of me in the hallway . . . ." Blaine continued to examine Callie's phone. "None of this is good, people."

Sunny went to Rocky, knelt down, and patted his back. He was still not himself and slumped back against the wall next to Tom.

"Oh this is good," Blaine said.

With each word, Sunny got sicker and sicker to her stomach.

"So, let me get this right. Callie sends a 'Safety Plan-packing list' to Sunny. It's a getaway list—photo ID, birth certificate, social security card . . . You got it all packed, babe?" Blaine glared at Sunny, then Callie. "You never should've stuck your nose in our business. Mistake of your life."

"Don't talk to her!" Tyson groaned.

Blaine dropped Callie's phone to the floor and, with a loud grunt, stomped it with the heel of his boot, just as he'd done to Sunny's foot. He repeated until he was out of breath and the phone was a rounded piece of mashed glass. Then he grabbed Tyson's phone from the coffee table and fired it against the small brick fireplace, smashing it into a dozen pieces.

Out of breath, Blaine wagged Sunny's phone at her. "We'll save yours for later." He slid it into his back pocket and stalked back toward the center of everything. He stood there, hands on waist, scanning the house, breathing hard, eyeing each person.

Sunny was afraid they would all die. It would become one of those bizarre news stories the whole country watched in horror, then forgot about.

Only Deetz could save them.

Look at all the weapons.

Blaine had a gun that Sunny assumed was Rocky's, stuck in the back waistband of his jeans. He had an assault rifle strapped over his shoulder. And Tom's and Tyson's guns were on the coffee table, unloaded.

"What's that I smell?" Blaine stepped into the kitchen. "Look here." He grabbed the carafe full of hot coffee and held it high above the sink. "What a shame it has to go to waste." Still holding it high, he poured the steaming dark liquid into the sink and Sunny's heart sank.

"You gotta watch Sunny. She's clever." Blaine clanked the empty carafe on the counter, crossed to a cupboard, moved some bottles around, and pulled down the dreaded Tequila, which never failed to bring out the worst in him.

Where is Deetz?

"Who wants a shot?" He came back into the living room waving the bottle and a shot glass. "Tyson, bet you could use one.

Ease the pain a little? What about you, officers? You're no longer on duty!"

Blaine laughed at his own joke, poured a shot, sloshing some on the floor, and threw it back himself. "Ahh." He walked over to the officers. Rocky was still out of it, but alive. Blaine poured another sloppy shot. "Put your head back," he said to Tom, who shook his head.

Just do the shot!

"You're gonna do this shot," Blaine said.

Tom shook his head no again.

Blaine leaned over him.

Tom sealed his mouth shut and clenched his teeth, determined not to open his mouth.

Blaine suddenly splashed the shot of Tequila onto Tom's open wound and he screamed.

Blaine leaned back and roared.

Sunny boiled inside. She kept thinking about the burner phone in her back pocket. It was up to her to *do something* before he killed them all.

"I'm going to the bathroom." She started to limp toward the hallway.

Blaine was on her in an instant, dropping the shot glass, which somehow didn't break, grabbing her arm, and shaking her.

"Don't tell me what you're gonna do!" He whirled her around toward the others and she let out a shriek. He shoved her hard to the floor next to Callie and Tyson.

Blaine froze and glared at Sunny. He stepped over to her, towering above her. "I heard something when you hit the floor," he said. "What's in your back pocket?"

Sunny's mouth dropped open and she shrieked in horror, but no sound came out.

Blaine reached down and jerked Sunny awkwardly, trying to flip her over. She fought against him with all her strength, but he easily overpowered her, grabbed her neck, and drove her face into the floor.

"Stop!" Tyson reached for Blaine's leg, but he kicked him away.

In a flash, he had Sunny's new phone. He turned it on and examined the screen.

"There's nothing on it," Sunny pleaded. "I haven't used it."

Blaine's face contorted and he threw the phone like a missile and it punched through the lower glass of the back door.

"Why is it I have a sneaking suspicion Wayne Deetz is on his way here? Huh, Sunny? Am I right, Callie?"

Callie and Tyson looked terrified.

Officer Tom's eyes were huge, but he was breathing hard, losing blood, slumping down further. Rocky, too, lay in an awkward position, in and out of consciousness.

Blaine took a swig of Tequila straight from the bottle and squinted. His eyes were bloodshot and glassy. He walked over with his huge metal-toed boots and the big chain swinging from his belt, and set the bottle on the kitchen table. Then he lifted the shoulder strap and swung the assault rifle around in front of him, grabbing it with both hands, as if he'd practiced it a million times.

"If that old cop shows up, he is *so* dead."

He pointed the menacing gun at Callie and Tyson and chuckled as they shrank back. He walked over to the cops and pointed it at them. Rocky glanced up at him with all the strength he had, but then slouched back down. Tom's jaw tightened and he glared at Blaine.

"What, tough guy?" Blaine approached Tom, who was sitting with his knees up, black shoes flat on the floor. Suddenly, Blaine stomped the top of Tom's left foot with a grunt. Tom yelled in agony, his eyes dancing with rage. But he was helpless, cuffed to Rocky, who was dead weight.

Without a word, Blaine spun around, headed into the kitchen, opened the far door, and went into the garage.

If they were ever going to talk it was in that moment.

"We've got to get out of here!" Sunny whispered loudly. "He'll kill us all."

"Run, Callie. Go!" Tyson said. "Sunny, go—now!"

Callie clutched Tyson. "I can't leave you. You'll die here! Deetz will be here soon."

"You girls, get out!" Tom said. "Rocky!" Tom shook the officer cuffed to him. "Rocky, man, we've got to *move*."

Rocky shuddered violently and tried to say something, but it was garbled.

"He needs oxygen." Tom shook his head, helpless. "Go girls, while you can!"

Sunny got to her feet and held out her hand. "Come on, Callie, now!"

Callie looked back at Tyson. He nodded quickly and pleaded with her to go.

Callie scrambled to her feet, took Sunny's hand, and they scurried for the back door.

A jarring gunshot blast shook the house.

Sunny and Callie dropped to the floor covering their heads.

Sunny looked back toward the kitchen slowly, half expecting to get shot.

Blaine stood there in a cloud of gun smoke, shaking his head, nostrils flaring. She'd seen that horrifying look a million times.

At his feet sat a large metal container of gasoline.

God help us.

The wind howled and the rain zig-zagged in every direction as Deetz drove down his driveway, his headlights reflecting off a mess of blowing leaves and branches that had fallen as a result of the night's storm. Instead of getting out in the rain to talk to the Portland PD officer parked at the curb, Deetz swung the Subaru around and pulled up right next to the cruiser. The officer rolled his window down.

"Thanks for being here." Deetz introduced himself as the rain sprayed both of them. "Did Virgil give you any background on the perp?"

The large shouldered Black officer nodded and peered over at the glowing computer screen on his mobile laptop. "Blaine Milligan. I was given a mugshot and description of his truck. Investigator Bennett said he may be armed and dangerous."

"He may be in another vehicle," Deetz added. "No one has any reason to come to the house tonight, so be suspicious of any car."

"You want me to block the driveway with my unit?"

Deetz liked the way this guy thought. "That's actually a great idea. Yes. Why don't you back in at the end of the driveway here."

The bald officer, James Nichols, nodded again. "I'll take care of it, sir."

"This guy's unstable and unpredictable. If he shows up, call for backup, immediately. And call me on my cell." They exchanged numbers.

"Have you heard about the tornadoes?"

Oh, great.

"No," Deetz said.

"Two EF-Zeroes popped up in the Hillsboro area, near Cornelius. We're under a Tornado Watch as of about three minutes ago."

"Sheesh. Thanks for letting me know."

One last time, Deetz urged the officer to contact him if anything seemed off, then he pulled out into the night.

Although he knew the way, he checked the map app on his phone. He was only nine minutes from Sunny's house. He did the math in his head and figured if everything went smoothly he'd be back home within an hour or two.

This is insane to be leaving Joanie.

He was too old for this, which he'd been saying for three years.

You always have an excuse to leave.

He thought about the huge trees that swayed in storms like this, right off their back porch. What if one fell?

Deetz had had it.

"This isn't right," he whispered.

You should be home.

Record numbers of officers and colleagues were retiring early due to the riots, attacks on police, and budgetary moves to defund the police.

He made a vow to go to HR and find out specifics about how much pension he would receive if he did retire early. He knew it would fall far short of the big bounty he was working toward for his thirty-five years of service. But he would get something. It was time he found out exactly how much.

He shook his head, feeling like a rookie cop who was over worked and under paid.

Joanie would break down crying with joy if he told her he was turning in the badge.

Maybe it's really time.

As prompted by the map app, Deetz turned on Sunny's street,

Demler Drive, recognizing it from the other morning when he'd squared off with Blaine Milligan. He cruised about a half-mile, through debris from the storm, and slowed as he approached Sunny's house. As expected, the Portland PD cruiser was backed in Sunny's driveway and Tyson's Jeep was at the curb in front of the house.

As Deetz continued slowly by, he realized the squad car was empty, which gave him pause. Although everything was probably fine, he continued driving slowly past the house. Several lights were on inside. He turned left on the adjacent street. A dark colored Ford Taurus was parked at the side of the road between Sunny's house and her neighbor's. Deetz cruised past, drove down the road, pulled into a driveway, and turned around.

Heading back the way he'd come, he eased to a stop behind Sunny's house.

There was no officer in sight in back of the house, either.

Deetz noticed the window where Tyson had put up the tarp after the Molotov Cocktail incident.

He watched the house, wondering if Sunny may've invited the officers in for something to eat, or perhaps they were using the bathroom.

But surely they wouldn't go inside at once.

After a moment, he continued driving. He swung around the Taurus and turned back onto Demler Drive, cruising slowly along the front of the house toward Tyson's Jeep. Since Sunny would have at least one suitcase and it was raining hard, he decided to pull into the driveway as close as he could get to the front door. He eased to a stop about six feet from the police cruiser, which he confirmed was indeed empty.

Deetz parked, turned off the car, got his phone off the dash, and grabbed the umbrella from behind the passenger seat. As he was about to plunge into the rain and head for the front door, he stopped. The empty squad car nagged at him, as did the fact that neither officer was visible.

Just to be safe, he called Tyson's number—but it went directly to voicemail. He eyed the front of the house through the rain. Lights on. No movement. He kept watching, double-checking in his mind that his gun was loaded.

The Taurus was bugging him, too. It was probably a neighbor's, but he wasn't sure of that.

Inside the house, the silhouette of a man's head leaned into sight ever so subtly, then back out of sight.

Uh oh.

With as little movement as possible, Deetz reached up, started the car, and backed down to the street. He stopped for two passing cars. He checked the house again. No one had come out, no one was in the window. With the street clear, he backed the Subaru into the road, put it in drive, and took off. He made the next right, planning to go around the block to the back of the house again.

Heart thumping as he drove, Deetz dialed Callie's number—it too went directly to voicemail without even ringing.

He's in there.

Deetz's head swam and he got woozy.

Breathe, man.

He leaned against the window and took several deep breaths of the cold, wet night air as he drove the block. It cleared his head.

He called Virgil's cell, but got his voicemail. "Virgil, Deetz. I need backup ASAP at Sunny Carlisle's house, Demler Drive, you have the address. Our PD cruiser's here but no one's in it. Tyson and Callie are inside and not answering their phones. I saw someone peering out. Could be Milligan, not positive. Have our guys come in quiet—no lights or sirens. Text me that you got this and are sending backup. I'm going to check it out closer from the back of the house. Tell the responding officers what's going on."

32

CALLIE WAS PRAYING SILENTLY for Tyson to hold on as she sat on the floor, propping his head up on her folded leg. He'd lost so much blood; the curtain was now soaked in it. His face was pasty white and washed in sweat, and his forehead was cold to the touch. "He needs to be at the hospital. Please," Callie yelled, "please let me take him."

"Shut up! Nobody move." Assault rifle in his big hands, Blaine moved surprisingly swiftly from the front room to the back of the house. "He's out there, somewhere. I saw him. Everybody, stay right where you are."

The way Blaine hurried from one window to the next suggested Deetz knew he was in the house; hopefully the cavalry would be arriving soon. Callie clung to that spark of hope.

Sunny sat on the floor leaning against the wall next to the back door with worry lines etched in her forehead. She knew Blaine better than any of them. Callie had the feeling she was probably thinking, if the police are coming, Blaine will take them all down with him.

But Callie refused to go there. She chose instead to think of massive SWAT teams and sharpshooters who could put an end to this nightmare with the squeeze of a trigger.

Officer Tom, whose uniform shirt was completely drenched in blood, had grown weak and was laying silently, awkwardly against the wall; his eyes opening and closing as if he was about to fall asleep—or worse. His partner, Rocky, had revived minutes earlier but was badly disoriented and claimed he could not see out of his right eye, probably due to oxygen loss.

They're no help. Tyson's no help.

She stared at Sunny and said, "Pray."

Sunny's head dropped in frustration.

The smell of fuel from the gas can in the kitchen permeated the house.

"Is Deetz here?" Tyson whispered, looking up into Callie's eyes, not moving his head.

"I think so," Callie whispered.

"When there's a chance, *run*. Get out." Tyson closed his eyes and wearily shook his head. "Don't think about me. Okay? Promise me."

Callie nodded.

"Promise," said Tyson, agitated.

"Okay . . . promise."

She would do as he said.

She would trust God to protect him.

But she knew if he didn't get medical help soon, he would die.

The window with the tarp was only about fifteen feet away. She figured she could run and dive through it if she had to, ripping it right off the nails.

"That old buzzard's gonna die, I swear." Blaine swung the assault rifle to his back as he moved to another window, yanking out his own big gun and racking the slide. "Old Joanie's gonna be a cop widow."

Callie made eye contact with Sunny, shifted her eyes to the back door, which was only feet from Sunny, and mouthed the word, "Run!"

Sunny shook her head curtly and mouthed something back that Callie couldn't decipher.

Callie guessed Sunny had said she would not abandon them.

In two strides, Blaine crossed to a light switch on the wall, smacked it off, and returned to the window. "Dang hurricane out there." He put a hand over his eyes and peered out at what sounded like hail pelting the tarp at the window near him.

Callie glanced back over at Sunny. She was stretched out, leaning over by the bottom of the door, looking through the hole in the glass.

Callie stopped breathing.

If Blaine saw Sunny peering out that hole, he'd throttle her.

"I should've kept one of those blasted radios." Blaine mumbled and cussed.

Quick as a cat, Sunny returned to her position sitting on the floor with her back against the wall, next to the door.

But the expression on her face had changed.

The whites of her eyes were big—clean and bright.

She bit her bottom lip as if deep in thought.

Did she see Deetz?

Have more police arrived?

They looked at each other and Sunny's eyes shifted to the hole in the glass at the bottom of the door, then back to Callie.

Sunny nodded slightly.

Her nostrils flared.

And she smiled, ever so slightly.

33

As Deetz slowly rounded the corner in the Subaru and approached the rear of Sunny's house again, the car shimmied from the massive wind, and hail pelted it in batches as if it was being tossed by the handful. Some of it came in his window.

Deetz realized nothing at all may be going on inside the house; he hoped that was the case. But why weren't the officers front and back like they were supposed to be? Why weren't Callie and Tyson answering their phones. Who was peering out?

His phone buzzed. A text from Virgil: "Two officers at Demler Drive not answering their radios. Unit en route to you. Be safe."

Thank God.

Deetz eased to a stop some sixty feet back from the dark Taurus, thinking he should've had Virgil run the tag number which, oddly, contained his own initials: WFD (Wayne Francis Deetz—Francis being the big family joke with the kids). He would have the officer run it upon arrival.

Deetz scanned the area. The two cops on duty were still nowhere in sight.

With the storm, it was possible Sunny invited them inside to post up in there, but he doubted it.

Lights had been turned out since Deetz had been back there earlier, and the interior was much darker now.

He noticed slight movement inside, but couldn't tell who it was.

His phone vibrated.

It was son J.P. calling. He had to take it.

All Deetz heard at first was massive chaos and J.P. practically screaming something unintelligible.

"Son. Son . . . Slow down. What's wrong?" said Deetz, whose head broke out in a sweat.

"Tammy got hit with a frozen water bottle—in the head. She's bleeding bad. It knocked her out for a minute. Now she's awake, but out of it," J.P. said. "Come on, Tammy—"

"Where are you?"

"It was supposed to be a vigil . . ."

"*Where?*" Deetz demanded.

"Courthouse—"

"J.P., why would you go there? Do you have a brain in your head? I could've told you what it'd be like down there; I warned you! Plus, there're tornado warnings—"

"Dad! I need to know what to do! Can you come? We're about to get trampled here. Should I call an ambulance? She's not right. She's out of it. She's not herself."

Dang it!

If Deetz had a normal job, he could go.

He examined Sunny's house. Another light flicked off. Still no officers.

"Where're you parked? Can't you take her to ER?" Deetz said.

"We took the TriMet," J.P. said. "It's pouring. Tammy, come on, babe, look at me."

"How bad's the gash?"

"It's gonna need stitches. It opened up her forehead, like two inches. It's bruising."

"Call an ambulance. Aren't there any cops around there who can help?"

All Deetz could hear was yelling and sirens and people bustling all around.

"J.P.?"

"I'll take care of it," J.P. said, frustrated. "Tell Brandon to stay away."

The call ended.

Deetz shook his head and smacked the phone on the seat in frustration.

Once again, he couldn't be there for his family. It drove him nuts.

What the heck are they doing out in this weather?

J.P. was going to have to put his big boy pants on and take care of it.

Joanie would want to know what was going on, but there was no time. If something was going down in Sunny's house, every second mattered.

Deetz silently surrendered Tammy and J.P. into God's hands, then focused back on the house.

He tried to clear his head, gather himself.

He unbuckled his seatbelt, climbed over and plopped into the passenger seat. He put the hood of his parka over his head, drew his Glock from its holster, racked the slide, and stared at the house a moment longer. "Protect me," he whispered. "Protect Sunny and Callie and Tyson—and the officers. Wherever Milligan is, bring him down, Lord, please. Bring him down *hard.*"

The backup unit would be there soon, but Deetz would scope it out in the meantime. He hoped to God by some longshot he was wrong about Milligan being in there; he would gladly serve as the laughingstock for the others when he showed up looking like a drowned rat.

He leaned his head back against the headrest, closed his eyes, and inhaled deeply. He held it a long time and exhaled slowly.

Then he opened the door and plunged into the storm.

34

Callie was sick with uneasiness. All color had drained from Tyson's face. He was barely staying awake; she had to keep urging him to keep his eyes open. They were to be married in the spring; her first genuine love. He'd lost his wife in the Portland shootings—and now she was about to lose him.

She squeezed his sweaty hand and leaned close. "Stay with me, big guy," she whispered. "Stay awake. You got this. Help will be here soon."

Tyson blinked and nodded.

God, help us.

"Everybody, stay down *low*, keep your mouths shut!" Milligan ordered, as he stood with his back to the wall near Sunny. "Anyone moves and you're dead. I got nothin' to lose here, so don't test me."

Tyson squeezed Callie's hand.

She looked down at him and his eyes were locked on hers. "Run," he whispered with all the strength he had.

She nodded, vowing to do just that when the right moment presented itself.

Periodic gales ripped at the tarp against the window, which had loosened and torn free at the bottom left corner. Cold air and the smell of rain whipped into the small house.

"I've got to go to the bathroom," Sunny said, looking up at

Milligan from her place on the floor next to the back door. "Please. I can crawl."

"No!" Milligan made his way along the wall to the adjacent window and peered out.

Callie examined Tom and Rocky from across the room. Both were slouched against the wall. A pool of blood had soaked in beneath Tom. Every few seconds his chest heaved. She was afraid he didn't have much longer. Rocky was alive. Every few minutes he would come to and babble something incoherent, try to get up, jerk his locked wrist against Tom's, then collapse in exhaustion.

"This guy . . . I swear." Milligan ducked back from the window, clutching the gun at his chest with both hands. He took another quick glance out the window, then said, "Stay *right* where you are," and bounded for the front room.

Callie looked over and Sunny was suddenly reaching through the broken window at the bottom of the door.

What are you doing?

Milligan was thirty feet away.

Should I run?

But Milligan had a clear shot at her. He turned off another lamp and carefully eased up against the front windows and looked into the night. Quickly, he ducked back and bent to one knee, debating what to do.

In two huge strides he was bending down over the two officers, wrestling with Rocky's utility belt. In a flash, he stood up with Rocky's handcuffs, eyed Callie, and headed toward her.

"No, please," Callie said. "I'm not going anywhere. I need to have my hands free to help him!"

Milligan just shook his head with jaw clenched, wrenched Callie's right wrist and locked it to Tyson's left. When he did, Tyson jerked awake, tried to take a swipe at Milligan, but realized his wrist was cuffed and dropped back to the floor in agony.

Callie finally broke down and began to sob.

Milligan laughed and stood, but remained hunched over. He petted Callie's hair and she squirmed in disgust. "I don't think you're going anywhere."

Then he took three giant steps over to Sunny and knelt down

next to her. "Now." He ran the back of a hand gently across her cheek. "We need to figure out what to do with you while I go outside and catch me a pig."

35

THE LENSES on Deetz's glasses were covered in rain and steam, and he could barely keep his hood up in the vexing wind. Someone had been looking out a window at the rear of the house, so he ran splashing into the side yard amidst the trees and ducked into some bushes right up against the side of the house, which had no windows.

He leaned against the house and caught his breath, wishing he'd worn boots; his lowcut leather shoes were caked in mud and his socks were drenched. The tall pines in the side yard swayed in the howling wind. He took off his glasses, put them up under his parka, and wiped the lenses with the front of his shirt.

His phone vibrated in his back pocket. With freezing fingers he put the glasses back on and grabbed his phone. Looking through the badly smudged lenses, he saw it was Virgil.

"What's up?" Deetz answered.

"Wayne, bad news. The unit I sent got mobbed by protestors right when it left the station. They're pinned in. It's unfolding as we speak, but it sounds like there are two hundred deep all around them. I don't think they're gonna make it to you any time soon."

Deetz started to ask for another unit, but Virgil cut him off. "I can't. I can't, Wayne. I'm sorry. It's mega-bad here. Every available uniform is on the streets. That's coming straight from the top."

"Even though we've got officers down here?"

"We don't know that."

Deetz went silent, weighing all his options for what to do next.

"One more thing, Wayne. We just got a call from a past victim of Blaine Milligan's—Brenda Marks. Milligan broke into her place early this morning. Tied her up. Cooked himself pancakes, eggs, and bacon. Drank two Bloody Marys. Then stole her car."

Deetz leaned his back to the house, looked back and forth and all around him. "Let me guess, dark Ford Taurus with WFD in the plates?"

"That's it," Virgil said. "Her sister found her tied up in the laundry room with a sock in her mouth and massive bruising on her neck."

"Virgil, listen to me." Deetz crouched lower and tried to keep his voice down. "Milligan is *in this house*. This guy's dangerous. Two of our guys—"

"The second I can get someone there, I will," Virgil said. "But you've got to understand what's happening right now in the city. It's mayhem like we've never seen before. We've got dozens of gunshot and knifing victims."

Squatting there in the rain, against the house, Deetz dropped his head in exasperation and tossed the phone back and forth in his hands.

Virgil rambled on in a tinny voice. Deetz looked down and punched the red button to end the call.

He took in a deep breath and stood.

Game time.

He'd done it a thousand times in his thirty-four years, and it was time to do it again.

He pocketed his phone, got out his gun, and crept slowly toward the front of the house with his back against it.

With each step, his heart rate increased.

With each step, he made sure he was breathing deeply and that his head was clear and alert.

He got to the front corner of the house, saw Tyson's Jeep at the curb and the empty squad car over in the driveway. The front lawn was scattered with debris. He ducked down and made his way to the first window. Slowly, he lifted up and peered in. There was a light on somewhere in the house, but the room he was looking in was dark; he remembered its configuration from when he'd been there the evening before.

Deetz backed away. The past two days had been a blur and he was running on fumes. He psyched himself up and looked in again. This time, the flash of a reflection caught his eye—on the floor. He cupped his hands to the screen and squinted.

A badge.

The reflection had come off a police badge.

Two officers were on the floor. All he could see was the outline of their bodies. One was moving. The other, still.

Dead?

Deetz fumed. He found himself breathing hard now, almost panting, and had to remind himself to stay cool, play it smart.

He ducked and scurried to the next window.

He caught his breath, lifted up, peered in.

It took him a few seconds to register what he was seeing.

There on the floor, just off the kitchen, bathed in fluorescent light—Callie was on her knees, leaning over Tyson, who was flat on the ground, covered in blood. Callie was pressing something against his thigh, a big bloody wad of something. At the same time, she was looking around the house, tense, her moves frantic. Her body was blocking Tyson's face, and Deetz couldn't tell if he was awake or not.

He dropped back down to a squat with his back to the house. The driving rain was coming sideways right at him, almost taunting him. He thought of Joanie and Brandon and Leena—and let out a sigh of relief. *At least they're safe.*

Next, he needed to get eyes on Milligan—and find out where Sunny was.

He eased up and looked in again.

From her position on the floor, Callie was looking up at something—something moving.

Deetz leaned out of sight but kept watching with one eye.

There he was.

Milligan.

His towering, hulking frame moved surprisingly smoothly as he crossed behind Callie and Tyson wearing black jeans and a white T-shirt—gun in one hand, assault rifle strapped to his back. He was in and out of sight in an instant.

Deetz's angle prevented him from seeing any more of the downstairs, so Sunny's location remained uncertain.

In the distance, beyond Callie and Tyson, Milligan came back into view. He was sneaking a look out one of the back windows.

Deetz dashed along the house, crept up to the front door, and gently tried the front doorknob.

Locked.

He quickly jogged past the garage to the other side of the house. Again, no windows on that side.

Good.

He made his way along the side of the house where the ground was wet and soft. As he thought through his options, he began sinking in mud, lost his balance, and went down—splat. His hands and gun sunk three inches into cold muck, and his knees did as well.

He plucked his hands out and stayed on his cold, wet knees, wiping his hands and gun on the front of his parka, cursing himself for being such an old klutz.

Leaning over on his right elbow, he grunted and worked his way back to his feet and stood there, unsteadily in the mud, looking for drier ground. He wiped his hands again and got his phone out to use the flashlight, but he couldn't make it come on because of the mud on his hands. He stuffed it back into his pocket and made a slippery leap right up against the house.

He got traction and stopped there.

It was pouring. He crouched down and rubbed his hands in a patch of wet grass and did the same with the gun.

His glasses dripped, making his vision blurry.

He was a *mess.*

An old man out in a tornado trying to stop a psycho.

He paused and shook his head at the mess he'd made of himself.

Then he looked around and shivered.

With careful steps, he walked right up against the house till he got to the back corner. He stopped and peered around the rear of the house. Two chairs and a table had blown into the small back yard and were rolling around under a big tree. Limbs and branches and leaves were strewn everywhere.

From what he could tell, closest to him was a bay window at the kitchen. Beyond that were two windows, one with the tarp flapping in the wind. Beyond that was the back door.

He crouched low and crept toward the kitchen window.

From there, he could see Tyson—whose face looked almost like a different person—clammy white, lips purple, opening and closing his eyes as if in and out of consciousness. There was a large puddle of blood beneath him and Callie continued to work on him. The house was too dark to see the downed officers and he did not see Sunny or Milligan.

But he did see a large, metal gas can, sitting in the middle of everything—a sober reminder of the irrational individual he was up against.

A real pyro.

Deetz inhaled deeply, held it, and blew a stream of steam into the cold night air. Then he bent down as low as he could and took off for the next window.

The big tarp over the window lashed in the wind and a lower quarter of it had come completely off its nails. Deetz could see right into the floor of the house. Over on the small concrete patio by the door sat a big waterlogged box of nails and two half-full Gatorade bottles rolling around in the wind.

Right up against the wall, Deetz lowered himself to the ground next to the opening in the window where the tarp was blowing. He peered inside, but couldn't see well. He wiped his lenses with his fingers to clear them. As the wind gusted, the tarp danced, giving him glances around the ground floor of the house. He was about ready to move to the next window when the wind whipped, the tarp flapped, and he saw Sunny's feet. He knew it was her because one shoe was bloody. She was sitting on the floor with her back against the wall, right next to the door.

In an attempt to see her better—determine what kind of condition she was in—Deetz pulled his hood off and leaned his head ever so slightly into the corner opening of the window.

There she was.

She looked good, sitting with her knees up. No wounds he could see. He followed her eyes—she was looking up in the direction right above his head. Then her mouth dropped open and her whole face contorted.

Uh oh . . .

Deetz started to back his head out and there was a sickening crack—to his head.

Searing pain.

Screams.

Blood.

Flickering lights.

His body and gun dropped into the wet grass.

He was violently hoisted up by the back of his raincoat.

Bumped into the house.

Thrown to the floor.

At the boots of Blaine Milligan.

36

———————

Sunny sat on the floor numb, her back to the wall, her mind in an altered state.

She'd watched Blaine standing stiff as a board next to the tarp-covered window with those maniac eyes dancing, waiting for his prey, as he'd so often waited for her.

With the crack of his gun to Deetz's skull, Sunny blinked, but that was it.

She couldn't feel anything. Didn't want to. *Mustn't.*

Emotion would interfere.

This is what Blaine Milligan did, he hurt people—inside and out.

Ruined lives.

Destroyed hope.

When Blaine hoisted Deetz up by his soaked jacket and threw him sprawling to the floor like a bag of bones, his big glasses broke and his head bled profusely. Callie screamed and Tyson cringed. But Sunny didn't flinch.

She surveyed the room—*her house*. A house she'd bought with her own hard-earned money. And it had been turned into a red light district hotel, bar, and lounge where this brazen freak breezed in and out any time he pleased.

She surveyed the downstairs soberly. Two people lay there

hemorrhaging, another fighting to take his next breath, and Callie—frantically doing all she could to keep Tyson alive.

Sunny was on auto-pilot.

In survival mode.

Glaring.

Observing.

Waiting.

Breathing hard, Blaine stood with his legs spread apart above Deetz. He leaned over and roughly patted him down. Deetz was unconscious. Blaine found his phone, tried and failed to turn it on, cussed, and fired it at the tarp. It hit and dropped outside. Then he crossed to that same window, leaned out, examined the ground, reached down with a grunt and retrieved Deetz's gun, which he must've dropped when he got clobbered.

Sunny had no concern about what weapons he had now.

None of that mattered anymore.

Blaine pointed the gun at Callie, then Sunny. "We're going," he said.

Sunny sat still, staring straight ahead, recalling with increasing heart rate the specific places throughout her peaceful little home where he'd turned it into a horror house. Beaten her bloody. Choked her till she passed out. And crushed the living spirit out of her.

It had all come down to this.

With her and him, it would end tonight; one way or another. She wasn't going to let it go on. No one else should ever have to face this savage.

"Sooner or later his cop pals are coming." Blaine bent down, unlocked Callie's handcuff, grabbed her left arm, and whipped her to her feet like a rag doll. She squealed in pain. Tyson looked up, helplessly, from the floor with his ashen face and half-closed eyes, his head shaking back and forth. All strength had drained from him.

But that strength was now in Sunny; the vengeance of every hurt person in that room roared in her head. All of the ways Blaine had tormented her were building up within her like a ticking time bomb.

Blaine glanced at her and said nothing as he made sure all his guns were safely secured in his waist band, and the big one, over his back.

He knows.

He sees . . . something is different this time.

Sunny saw that knowledge—that hesitance—flash in Blaine's black eyes.

As she sat there, counting the seconds with each beat of her thundering heart, she felt slightly out of her mind, deranged, like him. She chuckled in her mind, recalling when she worked in the tool department at the massive big-box store in Washington— seeing the exact item she'd just seen through the broken glass at the back door.

A howling massive gust of wind suddenly ripped the tarp right off the window and sent it floating into the night like a ghost. They all turned to look as rain gusted into the house through the eerie, black opening. Sunny heard trees creaking and the patio chairs clinking into each other as they rolled around in back.

"Get over here, Sunny." Blaine shoved Callie into a chair at the kitchen table and grabbed the metal gas can, fuel slurping to the floor.

Little did Blaine know of the inferno blazing in Sunny's soul as she sat there on the floor, unfazed by his demand.

He ignored that she hadn't obeyed, for the moment, and began dumping gas onto the kitchen floor and into the other room where Rocky and Tom lay unconscious.

With the sickening smell of gas filling the house, Sunny inched back slightly until she bumped the instrument she'd retrieved through the hole in the back door.

Hurriedly, Blaine continued shaking the heavy gas can, dousing the downstairs with petrol. He yelled at Sunny again to get over to him.

Sunny sat there like a revving drag car, engine thundering, combustion building, remembering the tool from the home store where she'd worked. It had been the most popular seller of its kind, because of its one-piece forged, polished steel head, unsurpassed balance, temper, comfort, and control.

Blaine threw the metal can across the room and began searching the kitchen, probably for matches. His lighter would be in his truck, where he smoked his smelly cigars. "Sunny. Get. Over. Here. *Now!*" he demanded.

Her insides blared as she sat there.

Terror and adrenaline plunged through her veins and pounded in her head.

He got that look on his face she knew all too well. Clenched jaw. Nostrils flaring. Eyes burning into her like lasers. He lurched toward her with giant strides, probably planning to rip her up by the hair.

"Sunny, do what he says!" Callie pleaded.

With her eyes locked on his, Sunny calmly reached around to the floor behind her and squeezed the bonded and molded, royal blue, nylon-vinyl shock reduction grip—guaranteed to reduce vibration by seventy percent.

Within four feet of her, his eyes flicked to the floor, where she was reaching.

"Come here, you *wench!*"

He leaned down and snatched her straight black hair.

"No!" Callie screamed.

In that instant, a menacing and piercing crack echoed sharp in the night, just beyond the open window.

They all froze.

Then came the cracking . . . and buckling. Loud and ominous.

Sunny could almost hear and sense the tree falling.

The enormous, stark, seemingly unreal pine tree demolished the corner of the house in a cloud of shingles, debris, and drywall dust.

Blaine dropped to the ground, his dark eyes huge as he cussed and stared in awe at the downed tree, open night sky, and rain now drenching the inside of the house.

That's when Sunny—with every trembling, surging, exploding ounce of pent up pain, disgrace, heartache, and rage—swung the twenty-eight-ounce milled-face framing hammer with rip claws in a sweeping arc in the direction of Blaine's large head.

She closed her eyes a half-second before impact.

For an instant, she likened the feeling to puncturing a watermelon—a brief rupture in the hard-half-inch rind, giving way to soft innards.

She let go of the hammer, her eyes shut tight.

His massive frame sprawled to the floor in a heap, one arm draped over her.

She scrambled out from beneath him and felt his pockets for her new phone, avoiding looking at the blood that certainly must be flowing.

She found it, frantically turned it on, dialed 911, and prayed to Callie's God that help would get there in time.

EPILOGUE

IT WAS A COLD, drizzly Thanksgiving morning. The sky was marble gray and Deetz was bundled up in his heavy winter coat and ski hat, sipping coffee next to his space heater on the back porch. He was able to see his breath in the frigid early morning air.

It'd been two weeks since the dreaded night at Sunny's house, where Blaine Milligan died from mass trauma to the head.

Deetz took his ski hat off and gently felt the bandage at the top of his own head, which covered a dozen stitches. He'd had to stay in the hospital for several days due to a concussion, and the doctors ordered him not to work for at least two weeks. He had an appointment scheduled for the upcoming Monday to determine if he was ready to go back to work—which had been the hot topic of discussion with Joanie ever since that night.

After about a week at home, he'd finally called HR at Portland PD to find out what his pension would be if he retired early—as in, never returned. It took them several days to get him the answer. The bottom line was, by retiring early—even by just one year—he would forfeit more than three-thousand dollars a month in retirement benefits.

Joanie had been fine with it. In fact, she'd been pressuring him the past few days to tear off the final ring on the paper chain she'd created that counted the four hundred plus days till he retired.

But Deetz hadn't made a decision.

Part of him was completely fed up and finished with police work, especially with all of the rioting and protests which continued downtown.

But part of him wanted to continue working, doing what he'd been called to do. Finish his thirty-five years. Get his full benefits package. Ride into the sunset with a solid nest egg. That kind of thinking infuriated Joanie. She made it crystal clear she wanted him to turn in his badge and be done with it, insisting they could make it on the reduced benefits package, their savings, and social security.

He planned to think and pray about it until Monday. It had even crossed his mind to let the doctor's decision be the ultimate verdict. So, if the doctor pronounced him in good enough health to return to work, that would be the sign he needed to finish out his thirty-five years. If the doctor said Deetz needed to take more time off, that would be the sign to turn in his badge—for good.

Joanie would think that was ridiculous.

For now, he would let it ride.

He smiled, put his hat back on, and rubbed his hands together close to the heater.

He was so thankful for Joanie. Thankful for the kids, for their beautiful home. Thankful just to be alive, especially after what had happened at Sunny's.

Regretfully, things hadn't turned out so well for Portland PD Officer Rocky Knollton. The choke hold Milligan used on Rocky had caused asphyxia. He'd faded in and out of consciousness until he sustained brain damage and fell into a coma. Today, Thanksgiving, he was in a 'permanent vegetative state,' leaving a wife and young daughter to fend for themselves.

Deetz sighed and felt his eyes fill with tears.

Thankfully, Rocky's partner, Tom Hood, survived. They'd done surgery that night to remove the bullet in his shoulder, followed by a second surgery a few days later to get bone and bullet fragments. Tom was in good spirits and said he was planning to return to work the following week.

Another light flicked on in the kitchen. Leena scurried about in her green plaid nightgown and fluffy white slippers, probably fixing her traditional morning breakfast of "toast toasted," with peanut butter.

The whole family would be coming later that day for turkey. They would stuff themselves, lay around, watch football, and feast on Joanie's famous pumpkin pie. J.P.'s girlfriend, Tammy, had suffered a minor concussion the night J.P. had called him from downtown, but she was fine. Deetz chuckled, thinking they could compare notes on their head injuries.

Leena opened the back door and stuck her head out. "Mom wants to know if you want breakfast. Sheesh, it's a frozen tundra out here. Why do you do this to yourself?"

He laughed. "Good morning. How's my sweet girl?"

"She's fine. Helping Mom. So, the answer to my question is?"

Deetz smiled. "Tell her no thanks."

"Copy that." She twirled around and closed the door.

They'd invited Callie and Tyson to come for the feast, but Tyson wasn't up to it. He'd only been home from the hospital for about four days and was still on antibiotics and keeping the leg elevated. Fortunately, the bullet that had pierced his thigh exited behind his kneecap without hitting bone. They air-flighted him to the hospital in the middle of the storm that night because they were concerned about his low oxygen levels and the amount of blood he'd lost. Once he got the care he needed, he stabilized. Callie said he was improving each day.

Sunny had not only agreed to come for Thanksgiving that afternoon, she'd insisted on bringing homemade cranberry sauce and marmalade candied carrots. That didn't exactly make Deetz's mouth water, but Callie insisted anything Sunny made would be off the charts.

Soon after the Blaine Milligan incident, Sunny not only got her roof fixed, but she had the same contractor redo all the floors in her house. When Deetz had called to invite her, she'd said the project had been a nightmare, but was finally finished, and she was thrilled with the outcome. It was a fresh new start for her, and Deetz could hear it in her voice.

The wind gusted into the porch. It was refreshing. He crossed his arms and closed his eyes.

Blaine Milligan had been one bad seed.

It's good he's dead.

Ever since the mass shooting at Pioneer Square several years back and the evil Deetz had seen in the teen shooter, Rogan Sneed, and in his accomplice, Willow Weston (a.k.a. Margo)—who'd kidnapped Leena—he'd done a lot of soul searching about evil and the old cliché—why bad things happen to good people.

The age-old question.

After much reading and watching online teachings, he'd determined two things. One was that God made everything for its own purpose—even the wicked for the day of evil. The other was similar, that God created vessels of *honor* and vessels of *dishonor.*

God did what he did.

It was up to Deetz to simply trust him.

There were wicked people out there, like Blaine Milligan, who, it seemed, were never meant to be good. They seemed to have a one-way ticket to hell, and their main goal along the way was to destroy as many lives as they could. The way Deetz read it—God had no plan to redeem them.

Did Deetz agree with that plan? Wasn't it cruel? Why would God redeem some and leave others on a path of destruction?

Deetz shook his head in silence.

He didn't understand it.

He wasn't sure he had it right.

It was difficult to understand such lofty things.

But whether he agreed or not with God's modus operandi really didn't matter. What mattered was, a few years ago he'd found an anchor of truth in the Bible, in God. Believing had changed his life —it'd given him sanity. It had given him someone strong and reliable to lean on. A powerful friend and father. When he talked to God quietly there on that back porch, confessed his faults, left his worries with God—he was free.

Thank you for that.

He was about to walk into that house, an imperfect human being, but with an unshakeable reassurance that, no matter what happened down here on earth, no matter how bad it got out there on his beat, he would spend forever with God in a paradise beyond description. All because God had said, *I Pick You.*

WHAT'S NEXT FROM CRESTON?

If you're ready to continue the breathtaking journey of Wayne Deetz and his beloved family, check out book four in the Signs of Life Series on **Amazon:**

ABOUT THE AUTHOR

Creston Mapes grew up in northeast Ohio, where he has fond memories of living with his family of five in the upstairs portion of his dad's early American furniture store - The Weathervane Shop. Creston was not a good student, but the one natural talent he possessed was writing.

He set type by hand and cranked out his own neighborhood newspaper as a kid, then went on to graduate with a degree in journalism from Bowling Green State University. Creston was a newspaper reporter and photographer in Ohio and Florida, then moved to Atlanta, Georgia, for a job as a creative copywriter.

Creston served for a stint as a creative director, but quickly learned he was not cut out for management. He went out on his own as a freelance writer in 1991 and, over the next 30 years, did work for Chick-fil-A, Coca-Cola, The Weather Channel, Oracle, ABC-TV, TNT Sports, colleges and universities, ad agencies, and more. He's ghost-written more than ten non-fiction books.

Along the way, Creston has written many contemporary thrillers, achieved Amazon Bestseller status multiple times, and had one of his novels (*Nobody*) optioned as a major motion picture.

Creston married his fourth-grade sweetheart, Patty, and they have four amazing adult children. Creston loves his part-time job as an usher at local venues where he gets to see all the latest-greatest concerts and sporting events. He enjoys reading, fishing, thrifting, time with his family, and dates with his wife.

To keep informed of special deals, giveaways, new releases, and exclusive updates from Creston, sign up for his newsletter at: **CrestonMapes.com/contact**

To view all of Creston's eBooks, audiobooks, and paperbacks go to **Amazon.com/author/crestonmapes**

STAND ALONE THRILLERS

I Am In Here
Nobody

SIGNS OF LIFE SERIES

Signs of Life
Let My Daughter Go
I Pick You
Charm Artist
Son & Shield
Secrets in Shadows

THE CRITTENDON FILES

Fear Has a Name
Poison Town
Sky Zone

ROCK STAR CHRONICLES

Dark Star: Confessions of a Rock Idol
Full Tilt